A CLEVER
DISGUISE

Other books in this series:

A Brilliant Deception

Other books by Kathleen Fuller:

Santa Fe Sunrise
Special Assignment
San Antonio Sunset
San Francisco Serenade

A CLEVER DISGUISE

•

Kathleen Fuller

Montlake
Romance

The characters and events portrayed in this book are fictitious. Any similarity to real persons, living or dead, is coincidental and not intended by the author.

Text copyright ©2008 by Kathleen Fuller
All rights reserved.
Printed in the United States of America.

Published by Montlake Romance
P.O. Box 400818
Las Vegas, NV 89140

ISBN-13: 9781477811542
ISBN-10: 1477811540

This title was previously published by Avalon Books; this version has been reproduced from the Avalon book archive files.

To my husband, James, for always being there.
I love you.

Prologue

April 1812

Emily Dymoke had almost completely and totally given up on love . . . until Gavin Parringer walked back into her life.

Her breath caught as the object of her affection threaded his way through the crush of people at the perimeter of the ballroom. He had come back. She hadn't thought she'd ever see him again, but there he was. In the flesh. The man she had fallen in love with over a year ago. The one she had thought she would have a future with. With him, she would live her very own happily ever after.

However, at the same time she had become besotted with him, he had fallen in love with someone else. And that someone else just happened to be her older sister, Diana, which made his unexpected appearance at Diana's engagement party most curious.

1

Emily's heart flipped and flopped as she watched him threading his way through the crush of partygoers. She couldn't take her eyes off his handsome form. He was tall—nearly a head taller than she—and a bit on the slender side, with a catlike grace and agility she had experienced firsthand the few times he had taken her for a turn on the dance floor. Truly, he was the most magnificent male specimen she had ever encountered. It had been easy to fall in love with him.

But having him love her back had turned out to be impossible.

She continued to watch, trying to tamp down the emotions clogging her throat, attempting to ignore the dampness of her palms beneath her white satin gloves. But when he approached Diana, Emily's apprehension spiked. The expression on his handsome face was intense, his body language rigid. He appeared ready for a confrontation, apparently not caring about the scandal it would cause her family or the black mark it would make on his reputation were he to disrupt the festivities. He was viscount—a fine position in society—and creating a fuss amidst a good many members of the *ton* wouldn't be easily forgotten.

Besides, he would ruin Diana's party and Emily couldn't permit that. She didn't always get along with her sister, but that didn't mean she didn't want her to be happy. Society and appearances were highly important to Diana. She would be crushed if a fete held in her honor ended up as fodder for the razor-sharp tongues of the gossipmongers.

Grasping the folds of her pale-pink ball gown, Emily hurried to the corner where Diana and her newly betrothed, William Garland, stood. They were speaking with a couple Emily didn't recognize, blissfully unaware of the approaching doom heading toward them in the form of Gavin Parringer. Providentially, Emily had been situated closer to her sister than Gavin, and she was able to step in front of him at the precise moment he opened his mouth to say Diana's name.

"Good evening, my lord," Emily said, extending a gloved hand, all while wishing the pounding in her chest would cease. She suspected he could see it thumping through the bodice of her dress. "I must say, I'm surprised to see you here."

"Miss Emily." Gavin took her hand dutifully and brushed the barest of kisses against her glove, then peered past her shoulder. "I wish to speak to Miss Diana—"

"She is otherwise engaged, Lord Tamesly," Emily said, ignoring the tingling sensation his lips left behind, despite the thickness of her satin glove. "I, on the other hand, am quite free. Would you like to sample the sweets at the refreshment table? Lily has assembled a delectable array to choose from."

Gavin ignored her suggestion, craning his neck as he tried to see past Emily. She remained firmly in his path, stepping toward him. For once her voluptuous figure, which teetered on the border of unacceptably plump, became her ally. She successfully blocked his line of vision. Her machinations served their purpose, forcing him to move further away from his goal. Finally, he tore his gaze away from Diana and looked directly at her. Desperation shone in his eyes.

A small measure of sympathy pricked at Emily, but she shoved it away. Any pain he experienced was of his own making, since he was determined to pursue a woman who had no interest in him, all while ignoring the one woman who would do anything for him. Including swallow her pride.

Deftly, she grasped the inside of his elbow and angled him away from Diana and William and toward the exit to the patio. "Would you mind accompanying me outside, my lord?" she asked, casting a glance over her shoulder at her sister. The couple remained unaware of Gavin's presence. "I believe I am in need of some fresh air."

His arm tensed beneath her hand, and for a moment she thought he would shrug her off. Then, to her surprise, he gave in and let her lead him away.

As they left the room, she caught a glimpse of her brother, Colin, handing a glass of lemonade to his wife, Lily. He whispered something into her ear and she laughed, touching her gently rounded belly as she did. Never had Emily witnessed a couple more suited for each other, or more in love. Lily's pregnancy had only cemented their close bond. Every member of the family anticipated the birth of the couple's first child.

Emily turned away from Colin and Lily and hurried her steps, not wanting her brother to notice anything amiss. He didn't need to see that his best friend had decided to crash the engagement party he had thrown for his sister. If he did, he might be compelled to say something. Or worse, do something. It would be much better if she handled this herself.

Of course, there was the added benefit of her and Gavin being alone.

They made their way to the back patio. The spacious area was unoccupied but well lit, so no one would suspect them of any improper behavior. Not that there was a chance Gavin would be improper toward her . . . no matter how much she wished it.

She turned and faced him. "I do not think you should be here, my lord."

His shoulders slumped as he turned away from her. "I suppose I shouldn't," he agreed with a dejected sigh.

"Then why did you come? What were you hoping to accomplish?"

"I had to see her . . . one more time. I have to tell her . . ." He tugged at his white cravat.

Emily watched as he swallowed his tension. Again she felt for him. He was clearly heartsick. "Tell her what?"

Gavin sighed heavily. "She doesn't love him. She cannot possibly love him."

Emily held up her hands, palms facing upward. "But they are betrothed. My sister wouldn't agree to marriage unless she loved her intended. She's always said she wants to marry for love." Despite her convincing words, however, Emily couldn't admit out loud that she'd had her own reservations about Diana's engagement. William was a gentleman and, although not a peer, he had the money and good reputation to make an adequate match for the older sister of a baron. There really was no reason for reservations about their relationship . . . other than the fact that they had known each other for only two weeks before William proposed.

"It happened too quickly," Gavin said, as if he were reading Emily's thoughts. He glanced at the patio entrance, as if he were contemplating a dash back into the ballroom. Emily breathed a sigh of relief when he remained in place. "I must talk to her. Just one more time . . ." A lock of his chestnut-colored hair fell over his eyes. Gavin had always been a jovial man, quick to make a clever quip or flash a charming grin. But his desperation over losing Diana had changed him to the point where he'd become a shadow of his former self. He looked weary. Lovelorn. Filled with unrequited love.

Emily knew the emotions well. Hadn't she experienced them a thousand times over the course of the last two seasons? She looked at him, and the layers of protection she'd built around her heart began to peel away. The hopelessness she had felt moments before disappeared, replaced with a feeling of anticipation. He had the power to do that to her, to make her forget she'd ever rejected the idea of love.

"I understand what you are going through," she whispered.

His head jerked in her direction as he glanced at her. "Beg your pardon?"

"I know how you're feeling." Against her will and all common sense, she found herself moving toward him.

"I know what its like to love someone who doesn't love you back."

He looked at her, his expression changing from weariness to wariness. "Emily . . ." he said, dropping all formality.

"Let me finish." She had to say the words. Had to tell him how she felt. They were alone, with nothing, and no one, between them. Boldly she looked him directly in the eye, compelled to speak the words she had never revealed to him, the ones she'd kept hidden deep in her heart. "I know how you feel about Diana . . . because I feel the same way about you. I love you, Gavin."

Shock filled his expression. "Emily—"

"I know you care for Diana—"

"I do not just care for her. I love her. With all my heart and soul, I love her."

His words pierced her straight through. With every word he dashed what little hope she had left. Still, she had committed to this unwise course, and she had to see it through. "She loves William," she said, stating the obvious. "She is going to marry him."

"I know!" he said sharply. Then he ran his fingers through his thick hair and moderated his tone. "I know she's engaged, Emily. Do you know how hard it was for me to come here? To see her with another man? To know that I cannot have her, no matter how desperately I want—no—*need* her?"

"Yes, Gavin. I do. I know exactly what you're feeling."

His expression immediately softened. He reached over and touched her shoulder, a gesture not unlike her brother would have done. "You are a sweet girl, Emily. I admit I have not been unaware that you had some sort of feeling for me."

Emily's lips pressed together at the casual way he spoke of her emotions.

"I am surprised you would tell me," he continued, "knowing how much I love your sister."

"Gavin—"

"Let me finish. You don't deserve this. You don't deserve me. I know you will find someone, Emily. Someone who can love you back."

"No!" she exclaimed, tears forming in her eyes. "I do not want to love someone else. I love you. I love only you." She grasped at him. "I can make you happy, Gavin, happier than Diana ever could. Please, just give me the chance. She cannot give you what you want, but I can."

He dropped his arm and stepped away from her. "I am leaving for India in the morning."

Her heart shifted to her feet. She hadn't expected this. "India?"

"Before long you will forget all about me." He turned to go, leaving her to stare at his back.

She couldn't believe what she was hearing. Did he really believe her feelings were so fickle? "Never! Gavin, please." She stepped toward his retreating form. "Listen to me. I can make you forget her."

He faced her again, giving her a patronizing half-smile that irritated her to her core. "Emily, be reasonable. What kind of relationship would we have, knowing that I love Diana? That I would see her and William at family functions and parties, and you would always be wondering if I were thinking about her, dreaming about her. I cannot do that to myself, and I will not do that to you. You do not deserve to be second best"—he paused, then added in a whisper—"I will never forget Diana." "She is the only woman for me. There can be no one else. Which is why I must go. Good-bye, Emily." Spinning on his heel, he moved to leave the patio.

"Wait!" she called out, embarrassed by the thick desperation in her voice.

Slowly he turned and faced her.

"Just tell me one thing, Gavin. And I want you to be completely honest."

He looked at her for a moment, then finally nodded.

The question perched on the tip of her tongue. She knew she shouldn't ask him, that posing her query would only bring more heartache. But she had to know. She couldn't let him walk away without giving her an answer.

She took a deep breath, then spoke. "Why Diana? What does she have that . . . that I do not? Why do you love her and not me?"

Gavin averted his gaze, shifting on his feet. His discomfort did nothing to lessen her desire to know his answer. She waited for him to speak.

Finally, he looked at her. Even though there was a distance between them, she could still read his expression, see the conflict in his eyes. "Emily, that isn't a fair question. I can explain my feelings for Diana to you, but what purpose would it serve?"

"Because I need to know!" She tugged on the fingers of the glove on her left hand. "Is it because I'm ugly? Because I'm . . ."—she choked down her embarrassment—"because I'm . . . fat?"

Gavin breathed out, the corner of his lips raising slightly in sympathy. "No, Emily. That could not be further from the truth. You are a lovely young woman."

"But not as lovely as Diana?"

Gavin didn't answer her directly. "Emily, I must go. Please give Colin and Lily my best for their babe." With that, he turned and walked away.

Emily swallowed her tears. They burned as they fell down her constricted throat. Emotions rushed over her like a wave rippling a lake. Devastation. Humiliation. Misery.

She had never stood a chance.

Never mind that he was right, at least about how difficult it would have been if they'd attempted a relationship. Even she wasn't deluded enough not to realize she would have spent the rest of her life being jealous of Diana, always fighting her for Gavin's affections. It would tear their family apart. She and her family had always been close, despite their penchant for the occasional spat between siblings, which often drove their mother to distraction. Emily knew she couldn't stand it if something—or someone—drove a wedge between them.

Yet hearing firsthand how she lacked compared to

Diana hurt. Emily had never been as slender and graceful as her sister. She'd always tended to be on the thick side, but in the past two years she'd put on more weight, to the point where some of her dresses were uncomfortably tight. Yet instead of attempting to lose the excess poundage, she felt compelled to eat more. Right now she wanted nothing more than to attack the refreshment table and consume a plate full of pastries.

But she held herself in check. Stuffing her face wasn't the answer. Unable to bear going inside and witnessing her family's happiness, Emily stepped to the edge of the patio. Soft tears slid down her face as she stared out into the inky darkness. She had bared her soul to this man, and he had rejected her. Never in her life had she felt so ashamed.

Suddenly, she paused as she detected the barest sound of rustling leaves nearby. Turning to her right, she saw a massive collection of thick, lush ferns, placed on small platforms of varying heights, decorating the darkened corner of the patio. She squinted as she saw a slight, shadowy movement. She wasn't alone after all.

"Hello?" she said, quickly wiping away her tears with the fingertips of her gloves. It wouldn't do for anyone to see her cry.

A tall, male figure stepped from the shadows of the corner. He cleared his throat. When he emerged into the light and headed toward her, flamboyantly overdressed and carrying a quizzing glass, she groaned inwardly. Just when she thought the evening couldn't have been any worse. Now she had to deal with Michael Balcarris.

Michael peered at Emily through his quizzing glass. If anyone had witnessed the two of them together, they would have seen a bored, overdressed fop giving a young lady a highly critical once-over. And that was exactly what he wanted them to see.

Inside, however, his feelings were quite the opposite.

In the flickering light of the oil lamps illuminating the patio, he couldn't help but take in the flush of her creamy complexion, or notice the glistening of unshed tears in her blue eyes. She was beautiful, even when she was upset. Having witnessed the exchange between her and that fool, Gavin Parringer, she had every right to be devastated. Parringer had no idea of the treasure he had in Emily.

Michael, on the other hand, did. He had for years now, every since he'd returned to London from one of his many trips to the continent. He hadn't seen her since she was an awkward fourteen-year-old. But she had been seventeen when he came back to London, and she had grown into a lovely young woman. As the years had passed, his attraction to her had only increased.

He adored everything about her, from her short temper to her enthusiasm for life to the dimple that appeared on her left cheek when she smiled. He couldn't believe she had called herself fat; she was far from it. He thought her the most prime-looking young woman in London, blessed with generous curves that might be considered too plump for the current fashion, but were perfect in his eyes. After seeing the pain in Emily's eyes, he wanted nothing more than to hunt Parringer down and pummel him for trampling on her tender feelings.

However, he could not indulge his impulses. He was powerless to do anything but stand there on the patio and play the role of Lord Hathery, cloying London fop. To reveal anything further, especially his feelings for Emily, would expose his secret—something he couldn't afford to do. He'd spent the past twelve years cultivating his outward persona, denying his identity, his emotions, his desires, all for the good of the crown. But at what cost to himself?

"What are you doing here, Michael?" Emily asked thickly. She crossed her arms defiantly over her chest— her usual stance when she was in his presence.

"Merely taking in the night air, Miss Emily," he said, forcing a light tone. "As I, ah, presume you are also doing."

She paled. "Dear Lord. You heard everything, didn't you?"

Before he could deny her words—which he had fully intended to do to spare her further embarrassment— she stormed toward him.

"How could you? How *dare* you eavesdrop on a private conversation?"

Because he would be expected to react in such an indifferent way, Michael shrugged, then glanced at his fingernails. "Perhaps you and Parringer should have picked a more private venue for your discussion."

"Oooh . . ." Emily radiated with fury. "You are a beastly man, Michael Balcarris, taking pleasure in someone else's pain."

"Oh, I assure you, Miss Emily. Your display was far from pleasurable. It was most tedious, actually."

Her bottom lip quivered. Here she was, in need of comfort and encouragement, and he couldn't offer it to her. It struck him to his core to say such things, to drive a verbal knife deeper into her already wounded heart. But he had to, despite wanting to take her into his arms and soothe her. It was well known throughout polite society that Lord Hathery possessed not a shred of compassion for anyone else. He cared nothing for anyone, except perhaps his mother, and at times that was even debatable. Many members of the *ton* dismissed him as a foppish twit, and that was what he needed them to think. He had no choice but to continue to fuel their assumptions.

Even when it devastated him inside.

Emily refused to give in to her pain, which had increased at an astounding rate upon finding out that Michael had heard her hand her heart to Gavin, only to have it shredded and tossed back at her. Instead she funneled her agony into an emotion she had a better handle on—fury. Lashing out at Michael was something she was used to, something she'd spent many a time doing. She detested the man in the extreme. However, soon her anger became too potent, and she couldn't speak. The last thing she needed—or wanted—was to be in the insufferable presence of Michael Balcarris.

Yet beneath her ire, she was still fighting her tears. To cry in front of Michael would only intensify the acute embarrassment she already felt. Better to stoke her heated emotions than to dissolve in a sobbing puddle.

"Ah, my dear Emily," he said, peering at her through that infernal glass he was never without. "Perhaps we should go back inside. Surely your mother has noticed your disappearance by now. Besides, I believe I hear the orchestra playing again. It would be my deepest honor to dance with you."

Emily clenched her teeth. This was classic Michael, completely clueless and without compassion. Apparently he wouldn't let her extreme stress over Gavin ruin his good time. Despite her never giving him the slightest inclination that she appreciated his company, he never failed to ask her to dance at every social event they attended. Manners often precluded her from refusing him, but this time she was throwing decorum out the window. The only thing worse than having to dance with Michael was listening to him talk. His conversation was emptier than the most vacuous of ingénues. Whenever he did have a decent comment to make—and those were rare moments indeed—it took him forever to expel it, as he tended to overenunciate everything.

Undaunted, he looked at her expectantly, forcing her to reply.

Instead of speaking she followed her instincts. She whirled around, turning her back on him.

"Tut, tut," Michael drawled. "Your answer is quite clear. I will take my leave, then. There are many other suitable females to dance with this eve."

She didn't respond, and waited for him to depart the patio. She shut her eyes tightly. Hopefully he would at least have the decency to leave her alone, without subjecting her to any of his absurd remarks. She felt a little relief when she heard his footsteps retreat from her.

To her amazement, a sudden stab of guilt pierced her. Yes, by refusing his request she had treated him a bit poorly. Later her conscience, formed by years of lessons in decorum and polite behavior, would force her to seek him out and apologize. But it would have to be at another time. She couldn't bring herself to be contrite tonight.

A spring chill filtered through the evening air. It not only cooled her body, it iced her heart. This was the worst night of her life. Forgetting about Michael, she mused on what she'd lost forever. Gavin. The tears she had tried so hard to keep at bay spilled down her cheeks. Any hope of a future with the man she loved died when he left.

Chapter One

June 1812

Emily stood on the perimeter of the ballroom, watching beautifully attired women and dashing, handsome men swirling and gliding on the polished wood floor. It was the last party of the season, thrown by Michael and his mother, the dowager Countess Hathery, and by all accounts it was the finest fete of the year. Yet Emily couldn't bring herself to enjoy it.

She didn't want to be here.

She stifled a yawn, unable to enjoy any of the festivities. Even the promise of a spectacular fireworks show at the end of the evening couldn't pierce her apathy.

She spied Diana. Not surprisingly, her grace and beauty radiated throughout the room. Her fiancé, William, held her close in his arms as they danced. The barest hint of envy pricked her. It was easy to dismiss, just as it was becoming easier to put Gavin out of her mind.

She had finally stopped imagining and thinking about what could have been and had accepted reality. It was over. Gavin was in India. No one, not even Colin, had heard from him. Now she was here at Michael's, bored out of her mind.

Emily sighed. She truly hated parties now, since there was no point in her being here. Although she was of marriageable age and her mother had made certain everyone knew she was on the market, gentlemen had stopped approaching her. Not that she had an overabundance of men interested in her. She'd always been a bit self-conscious about her rounded curves, and had sympathized with her sister-in-law, Lily, who was tall and exceptionally thin. Being physically different from the current fashion could at times be a bitter pill to swallow.

But over the past couple months, since her last encounter with Gavin, she had developed such an irritating persona that the few men who did approach could barely stand to put up with her. She wasn't out-and-out rude, but she never made an effort to engage in conversation, limiting her answers to three words: *yes*, *no*, and *indubitably*. She had refused to entertain visitors other than her sister-in-law, and only accepted party invitations when her mother forced her to, such as tonight's tedious soiree. This didn't endear her to any possible suitors, and her unpleasant behavior had driven her mother to near apoplexy.

Out of the corner of her eye she saw Michael, which caused her to clench her gloved fists. She had long ago apologized to him for her behavior the night Gavin had broken her heart. Unfortunately he had taken that as an open invitation to seek her company at any public events where they were both in attendance. He was approaching her now, no doubt on a mission to ask her to dance yet again. She wasn't surprised that he was making his way over to her, but she had merely hoped he wouldn't have seen her until later in the evening, when she could have feigned a stomachache or some other malaise. Even she didn't have poor enough form to leave a party so shortly after arriving.

"Ah, Miss Emily," Michael said, taking a deep bow. "Mother has outdone herself tonight, do you not think? I do hope you are, um, enjoying yourself."

"Yes," she muttered.

"Yes, what?"

"Yes, the countess has outdone herself," she gritted out.

Michael arched a perfectly shaped brow. He had the most fastidious grooming habits of any man she'd ever met. "Is that all you can think to say? My darling Emily, perhaps you should learn to expand your vocabulary a little bit."

"Perhaps you should keep your paltry insights to yourself."

Instead of being offended by her biting tone, he merely chuckled. "Charming as always, I see. Ah, I hear the orchestra is starting another tune. Shall we dance?" He bowed slightly at the waist and held out his hand.

Knowing to refuse her host would be rude in the extreme, and considering there were several witnesses around her to see her make such a socially deadly faux pas if she did tell him no, Emily reluctantly placed her gloved hand in his limp one. He barely held it as he led her on to the dance floor. His other hand at the back of her waist remained just as flaccid.

She prayed the song would be a short one.

They danced in silence, Emily taking care not to look at Michael too much. His foppery made her queasy. Not only that, his mere presence still reminded her of that night two months ago, when he had witnessed her ultimate humiliation. Thus far he had the good grace not to mention it.

Finally she had no choice but to look at him, as she had forced her gaze on everything in the room but him. There was one thing about Michael no one could deny. He had the potential to be a very good-looking man. He had the most astounding green eyes. They were definitely his most-arresting feature. The rest of his countenance was quite winsome. He had a nicely shaped nose, a strong chin, and perfectly straight, white teeth. These characteristics had been particularly attractive to her when Michael had been younger, before he left London to attend university. Her mother and his mother were the best of friends, and as children, he and Colin played together, with Emily lagging behind, trying to keep up. Diana had had no use for such boyish nonsense, but Emily had enjoyed their roughhousing and adventures tremendously. In Michael, it was as if she had a second older brother. At least at the time it had.

Then it happened, the moment she'd seen him as

more than a brother. She was fourteen and he was seventeen, and getting ready to leave for Oxford. One of her cats, Periwinkle, had chased a bird up a tree and became too frightened to come down on her own. Emily had climbed after her, only to have Periwinkle claw her way further and further up the branches. Emily was halfway up the tree before she looked down. That had been a huge mistake. Terror had filled every inch of her being, and she'd clung to the tree for her very life.

That was how Michael had found her, hanging from the branches, hair and dress askew, trying not to dissolve into terrified tears but losing the battle with each passing minute. He had called her name only once before scaling the tree with quick, athletic grace. She could still remember the strength of his arms as he'd drawn her close to him and helped her down the tree. When they reached the ground, he didn't tease her or scold her or threaten to tell her mother that she'd done such a foolish thing.

Instead he just looked at her with genuine concern and asked her if she was all right. He had touched her cheek for the briefest of seconds with the tip of his index finger, then went back up the tree and rescued her cat.

Her young heart had been mesmerized. She had never realized before then how handsome he was. Or how caring. She watched as he gently picked up Periwinkle and cradled her in the crook of his arm. He handed Emily the cat, giving her an encouraging smile. "Next time," he'd said, "fetch me before you decide to play the heroine. You could have been hurt." Then he'd walked her back to the house, not ever knowing how smitten she'd become with him.

However, that was then and this was now, and any appeal Michael might have possessed was ruined by the way he sucked in his cheeks and pursed his lips, and how he viewed everyone and everything through a filter of boredom. The worst part was he didn't realize that he topped the list of the most boring things in society. She missed the adventurous, amusing, and fun-loving Michael she used to adore. For some unfathomable reason that no one knew, he had changed from a robust man to a limp-wristed dandy.

Such a waste.

"You are quite pensive, Emily," he drawled.

His voice drew her out of her thoughts. "I beg your pardon?"

"Usually you are chirping away about some utter nonsense or whatnot. But lately you have been rather, ah, dreary."

"Michael, you are the last person who should be giving a lecture on scintillating conversation."

"I am merely saying—"

"And I wish you would merely shut up!"

The sharpness of her tone seemed to affect him, and he acquiesced to her wish. For the rest of the dance he didn't say another word.

Soon providence intervened and the orchestra finished their song. "There," she said. "I have done my duty for the night. Now if you will excuse me." She whirled on her heel and headed for the balcony, away from the insufferable Michael Balcarris and the happy couples that seemed to fill every square inch of the ballroom.

Michael sighed inwardly as he watched Emily storm off. It was becoming harder and harder for him to keep up his ruse. Tonight was no exception. He didn't know why he continually asked Emily to dance. He knew she detested him. Yet he couldn't resist the chance to hold her in his arms for at least a few minutes. It was sweet torture—not only because he couldn't tell her the truth about his life and his feelings for her, but also because she held him in such contempt.

Only three other people knew his secret—his trusted colleague, Clewes, who had been his mentor throughout his career as a spy, his best friend, Colin, and Colin's wife, Lily. They were his closest—no, his only—confidantes, and had proved beyond trustworthy. But soon he would have to make a decision. He couldn't go on living a double life: Michael Balcarris, effeminate fop, and Michael Balcarris, British spy.

But tonight wasn't the time or place to ponder his future. At the moment he was more concerned about Emily. In his necessary rude way he had alluded to the sadness that seemed to consume her. She had changed so much in the past two months, and not for the better. Gavin Parringer definitely had something to do with her mood. The man was an imbecile to deflect her feelings, but at least Michael was spared dealing with the jealousy that would undoubtedly rear up at the knowledge that Emily was with someone else. True, he couldn't have her, but if he was honest with himself, he didn't want anyone else to either.

Still, he would have suffered anything if it meant Emily's happiness.

The orchestra started playing again, leaving Michael alone on the dance floor surrounded by other couples. He deftly sidestepped a few of them and headed for the balcony, where Emily had darted a few minutes earlier. He was well aware that his interference could set her off all over again. However he stayed his course. When it came to Emily, his common sense seemed to go on holiday.

He stepped onto the stone balcony, his breath catching at the sight of her, as it always did. Quietly he crept toward her.

She whipped around and faced him.

He jumped back a little, surprised at her impressive sense of hearing.

"What do you want now, Michael?" she said, her tone more weary than combative.

Michael lifted his quizzing glass, giving himself time to collect his thoughts and reinforce his disguise. "As I stated before, dearest Emily, you seem to be out of sorts."

"I fail to comprehend why my mood is any of your business." She turned her back to him.

He moved until he was standing next to her. "Seeing as this is my party, I do believe it is my business to make sure that my guests are content."

"I am content. Now go."

Well, this was going swimmingly. He marveled that

as a spy, he'd been able to interrogate some of the most jaded of French spies, gleaning information out of them before they realized they had revealed anything. But when it came to talking to Emily Dymoke, he was completely flummoxed.

"Have you tried the refreshments?" he asked lamely, fighting the urge to roll his eyes at his own pitiful banter. Here she was nursing a broken heart and all he could offer her were teacakes.

"I am not hungry." She turned to him. "Nor am I thirsty. I do not want to dance, or talk about fashion, or gossip about the latest scandal rocking the *ton.* What I do want, my lord, is to be left alone. I would appreciate it if you honor my request."

"I hardly think that is a prime idea, for I can see you are clearly upset. I pray I am not the cause of your distress?"

Emily scrunched her eyes shut, and Michael could have sworn she was counting to ten. She opened them, her blue eyes sparking with fire.

Michael steeled himself against the wave of attraction flowing over him. She was beautiful even when she was angry, with her cheeks flushing pink and her lips in a fiery pout. He would have given his left arm to kiss her pert mouth right then and there. He could only imagine how soft it would feel. Instead he had to feign placidity, and it was nearly killing him.

"You well know the cause of my distress, my lord, considering you were in the foremost of positions to witness it." "But since you brought the subject up, Michael, let me assure you that you are *always* a source of consternation." Her tone was reminiscent of a mother giving her naughty child a complete dressing down. "It boggles my mind that you have not realized it. Your airs are pretentious, your wardrobe preposterous—"

"Is everything all right here?"

At the sound of the masculine voice, both Michael and Emily turned at the same time. An unfamiliar gentleman stood at the balcony entrance, a concerned and bewildered expression on his face. Michael didn't recognize him as a regular of the peerage social circuit, but he also hadn't been privy to his mother's complete guest list.

"Everything is fine," Emily said, her words meant for the stranger but giving Michael a hostile glare. "Lord Hathery and I were just having a spirited conversation."

"Which of course, is nothing out of the ordinary," Michael concurred.

The man looked from Emily to Michael, then back to Emily again, as if he was considering whether to believe them or not. Finally, he said, "I am sorry to have intruded. Please allow me to introduce myself. I am Charles Pembrooke. I am visiting my cousin here in London, Lord Mumblethorpe."

Michael introduced Emily, then himself. "I was not aware Mumblethorpe had any cousins," he said.

"Distant cousin, I assure you. Twice removed. We only met for the first time a fortnight ago."

Michael was tempted to test the man's story by seeking out Mumblethorpe himself, but he dismissed the idea. The poor earl was not only hard of hearing, but a bit addled. Michael doubted he would be able to answer questions about Pembrooke with any accuracy.

With one swift, smooth movement that had surprised both Michael and Emily, Pembrooke grasped her hand and lightly kissed her gloved fingers. "Lovely to meet you, Miss . . . I am sorry, could you tell me your name again?"

"Dymoke," she said, sounding oddly breathless. Her attention was completely turned away from Michael at this point. "Emily Dymoke."

Something ugly twisted inside Michael as he noticed the singular attention Emily and Charles paid to each other, as if Michael had disappeared into the stonework of the balcony. Normally being ignored by others didn't bother him. It gave him the opportunity to be covert in his observations. But not this time. Emily's nonverbal dismissal of him grated.

"If I may be so bold, Miss Emily, could I have the next dance?" Pembrooke asked, his gray eyes never leaving hers. Then he turned to Michael, as if just remembering he was still there. "If it is agreeable to Lord Hathery, of course."

Emily lifted her chin, giving Michael a defiant glance, as if daring him to comment on her choice of dance partners. At that moment Michael knew what her answer would be, and he didn't like it one whit.

She turned back to Pembrooke, her eyes holding more interest and life than Michael had seen in weeks. "I would be most pleased to dance with you, Mr. Pembrooke."

Charles grinned. "Splendid, then. Shall we go?"

Without casting Michael so much as a glance, Emily put her hand on the crook of Pembrooke's arm and allowed him to lead her from the balcony.

Once Emily was out of sight and probably firmly ensconced in Pembrooke's embrace, Michael stiffly swirled around and looked out over his mother's garden, trying to stem his growing jealousy. The emotion gnawed at him, causing him tangible pain. It was all so very irrational. Absolutely ridiculous.

And completely tiring.

He couldn't go on like this. It was high time he rid himself of his feelings for Emily Dymoke once and for all. He didn't have the time or the energy to deal with them. The truth was they weren't worth dealing with most of the time, as she made her distaste for him abundantly clear.

There was only one problem, however.

How exactly did one fall *out* of love?

Chapter Three

To Emily's surprise, Charles was a lovely dancer. He was also handsome, charming, and a brilliant conversationalist. He didn't drone on and on about the intrigues of the *ton*, or how many waistcoats he had, or how splendid the gentleman's club White's was, and what a pity she couldn't find out for herself, as women weren't allowed to darken its doorstep.

Instead he admired her sapphire necklace, complimented her dancing, and flashed an engaging smile that had undoubtedly charmed the satin gloves off many a young ingénue. In many ways he reminded her of Gavin. He even resembled him physically, down to his slender frame and unruly brown hair. Their eye color was pretty much the only thing different.

Still, for all his attributes, Charles wasn't Gavin. In her mind, he was irreplaceable.

"Have I said something to offend you?" he asked suddenly, drawing her out of her thoughts.

She quickly looked at him again, forcing herself to pay attention to him. It wasn't his fault she was still having trouble forgetting about Gavin, and he didn't deserve to be ignored. "No, not at all. I apologize for making you think that you have. I fear I have been rather preoccupied tonight."

"With Lord Hathery?"

She chuckled a bit at the ridiculousness of his question. It was the first time she'd been able to smile in quite a while. "Oh, dear heavens no. I shoved him out of my thoughts a long time ago." However, she did make herself a mental reminder to apologize to Michael yet once again. She had been shrewish to him for the umpteenth time. For some reason, he always seemed to bring out the worst in her. Still, that was no excuse for her poor behavior toward him. She needed to learn to keep her temper and sharp tongue in check—even in the presence of Michael.

Charles twirled her around the corner of the ballroom floor with precision. "So you and Lord Hathery are not together then?"

Emily laughed out loud this time, her first genuine laugh of the evening. Actually, her first laugh in what seemed like forever. "Of course not. I can barely abide the man. He is a family friend, nothing more. Actually to call him a friend would be stretching reality quite a bit."

Charles appeared relieved. "I am glad to hear that. I

had just assumed since you were alone on the balcony together that I had intruded on a private moment. It is nice to know that my assumption was wrong." He smiled at her again, drawing her closer to him. It was a bold move, one that should have made Emily's heart leap just a little. But it didn't. Oddly enough, she didn't feel anything at all.

If he noticed her lack of response, he didn't let on. "Forgive me for being presumptuous," he said, as the music filtered through the air all around them. "I know we have only just met, and I do not mean to make you ill at ease, but . . . could I gain your permission to call on you this week?"

She blinked. This was most unexpected, especially since he was the first man she'd met at one of these events she hadn't known for years, or at least had known his family. She had only thought they would dance, nothing more. "I—I . . ."

He guided her around once more. "A thousand pardons if I am overstepping my bounds, Miss Dymoke. I will admit to being a bit on the impulsive side at times. But if you prefer I do not visit you, then I will respect your wishes."

He really was a most polite man, a quality she appreciated in people, despite her own personal struggles with courtesy. And she couldn't think of a single reason why he couldn't call on her. Not one that would make sense anyway. She had spent the last couple of months refusing suitors, and her reticence to entertain anyone was driving her mother batty. Perhaps now was the time to get back in the game, so to speak. "Yes, Mr. Pembrooke. I would be happy if you called on me."

The music stopped to polite applause as his face broke out in a wide grin. He led her off the floor and bowed deeply, then rose and met her gaze. "Thank you, Miss Dymoke, for the dance. I thoroughly enjoyed it, and I hope you did too. I look forward to seeing you again. Very soon." Smiling one last time, he slipped away into the crowd, leaving her alone with her bemused thoughts and emotions.

Away from his charms, she was able to think a little more clearly. What had she done? She had just agreed to see Charles again, a man she really had no interest in, even though he did seem to possess a gift for putting her at ease. Now she had more than a niggling of regret that she had answered him in the affirmative, as she wasn't sure she was truly ready to have a suitor. His eagerness had come as a surprise too. She had been used to most gentlemen putting forth polite interest, almost as if interacting with her had been a duty instead of a pleasure. And she supposed it probably had been, considering she wasn't exactly a prime catch, especially in light of her figure flaws and the vinegary temperament she'd been displaying recently.

Yet she couldn't ignore the fact that a part of her was flattered by such extreme attention by a handsome stranger. That was an experience often reserved for Diana, not her. Maybe Charles would give her the final push she needed to get out of her quagmire of grief over losing Gavin. The thought made her smile slightly.

When she retreated from her thoughts, she realized she had been left alone on the dance floor, as everyone had departed for the Balcarris garden and the ensuing festivities. Standing on her own in the middle of the ballroom wasn't exactly an enviable position for a young lady. Gathering her composure, she followed the rest of the crowd. A sense of anticipation radiated from the people around her, intruding on her confusion.

The fireworks were about to start.

Michael remained on the edge of the garden apart from the rest of the guests and watched the fireworks. Some of the ladies and gentlemen had huddled onto the balcony, but the majority of people were outside in the garden itself, eagerly anticipating the show. His mother had wanted to throw the ultimate party to mark the end of the season, and she had. The colorful explosives were the crowning touch.

Having spent time in the Orient, fireworks were hardly a novelty for Michael. But he enjoyed the excitement filtering through the crowd. He saw Colin and Lily standing together, his arm wrapped around her waist, which had thickened slightly from her impending motherhood. Not too many people knew she was expecting, as the couple had wanted to keep it a secret from everyone except for close family and friends. He smiled, happy for them both. They were a well-suited couple, a fact he had recognized before either of them had realized it.

Two years ago Lily had been framed as a thief who had pilfered the *ton* of their jewels, particularly bracelets. The unfortunate incident had brought Colin and Lily together when they had banded to clear her name. Because Michael had been trailing the same bandit, he had been forced to reveal his secret to the two of them and become involved in the apprehension of the criminal. Having been close to Colin for years, Michael had known early on that Lily was perfect for Colin. It had taken his friend a little longer to come around, but now they were one of the most solidly in love couples in London.

Michael continued to scan the crowd, spying Colin's mother, his sister Diana and her fiancé, William, along with his own mother, all talking with Lady Hartford. However, he didn't see Emily anywhere. He fought the strong urge to look for her. He had made a big enough fool of himself in her presence already. He rather preferred not to be on the receiving end of any more of her vitriol.

His thoughts moved on to Charles. Michael had briefly witnessed him dancing earlier with Emily. She appeared to be enjoying herself, something she never did when dancing with him. He had forced himself not to dwell on it. A beautiful woman like Emily would soon find someone to share her life with. The faster he accepted that, the better.

But knowing what he had to do didn't make it any easier to accomplish.

The fireworks began, exploding in the air in a riot of light and color. Vibrant blues, reds, greens, and blinding whites glittered against the black sky. Michael listened to the crowd express their awe and appreciation of the display. Their response would undoubtedly please his mother. He glanced at her, happy to see the gleeful expression on her face.

Then out of the corner of his eye, he spied Emily, standing next to Millicent Abernathy. She was so beautiful it made his heart hurt. The illumination of the fireworks reflected an expression he hadn't seen on her face in a very long time. One he wished he had caused, but knew he never would.

She looked happy.

Chapter Four

"So how are things in the spy business?" Colin poured Michael a glass of shimmering port, then handed it to him.

Michael accepted the drink. They were in Colin's study, the door locked to ensure their privacy. Michael loosened his cravat and leaned against the wine-colored, high-backed chair. His friend's comfortable study was one of the few places he felt free to relax and be himself.

"As to be expected." Michael swirled the dark liquid in the glass. He brought it to his lips and took a sip, feeling the warmth of the wine slide down his throat. "In fact, there has been a lull of intrigue as of late."

Colin prepared a drink for himself then sat down at his desk. "That's good to hear. It must mean London's more nefarious elements are behaving themselves."

"I seriously doubt that, but one can hope." Michael took another swig, then regarded his friend contemplatively. "Certainly you haven't asked me here to see if I have any assignments for you, mate. Because even if I had one to give you, I would not. You do not need to be gallivanting around pursuing criminals. Not with Lily in her current delicate condition."

"You are absolutely right. I am not interested in any intrigue, to be sure. At the moment I am much more concerned with things on the home front."

Michael leaned forward, concerned. "Is Lily having difficulties with the pregnancy?"

"No, fortunately. But I will admit she's changed. Oh, I still love her to bits, but something about being pregnant has set her on edge and makes her cranky. At times she is almost unbearable to be around."

"I do not think that is uncommon with expectant mothers."

Colin nodded. "Mother says she was the same way when she was expecting. Believe me, Michael, that was a conversation I would rather not repeat. Women have a tendency to share more information than necessary, especially when it comes to pregnancy and childbirth."

Michael laughed at Colin's appalled expression. "I do not envy you having to listen to that." Quickly, though, his mood suddenly turned somber. As much as he wouldn't have wanted to listen to Colin's mother's monologue on giving birth, there were plenty of other things about Colin's life Michael did envy. The man's freedom, for one. Colin occasionally helped Michael with small

missions in London, but his friend didn't have to culti-
vate a disguise to hide behind. No one would ever expect
the dapper Colin Dymoke, Baron of Chesreton, a spy.
Which made him a perfect partner, one Michael would
trust with his life. But Colin would always be free to be
himself. He wouldn't have to deny his true nature . . . or
his feelings for the woman he loved.

"Lily would be mortified if she knew we were discussing her in this fashion," Colin said, taking up his
own glass of port and sitting across from Michael. "I
believe we should probably drop the subject posthaste."

"I agree," Michael said, appreciating Colin's respect
for his wife.

"Besides, Lily isn't the reason I invited you here. I
wanted to ask for your help."

"Anything," Michael said, listening intently.

"What do you know about Charles Pembrooke?"

Michael gripped the side of the glass and shifted in
his seat. If Colin felt the need to ask Michael about
Pembrooke, then Emily most likely had to be involved
in some way. "I do not know much about him. He mentioned he was a cousin of Lord Mumblethorpe, but nothing else of import. Actually, I had never seen him prior
to the other night. Why do you ask?"

Leaning back in his chair, Colin set his drink on his
desk, his expression somber. "I saw him dancing with
Emily the other night at your party. I didn't think anything about it, I simply figured she had finally decided
to give a chap a break for once. It wasn't until Mother
mentioned that he had asked to call on her that I be-

came concerned. He has become smitten with her, a little too quickly, I think, especially considering he is apparently new to London. I will admit to being surprised that she agreed to his request. She hasn't entertained any suitors in a very long time. I will admit that part of me is glad that she is getting over Gavin, but I wish it was with someone I knew. Thus I want to find out what I can about him. After the debacle with Gavin, I do not want anyone else hurting her feelings."

"I didn't realize you blamed Gavin for what happened with Emily."

"Oh, I don't. I knew what Gavin felt for Diana before I found out that Emily liked him too. It is just that Emily tends to be a bit . . ."

"Impulsive?"

"I was going to say reckless, but impulsive fits as well." He looked at Michael. "I want to make sure I know who I am dealing with when it comes to Pembrooke, in case things turn serious between him and Emily."

Michael didn't like the sound of that at all, but he had to face reality. Emily wouldn't remain single for too much longer. She had far too much to recommend her as a wife: intelligence, beauty, a substantial dowry. He thought Colin made a responsible decision to have the man checked out. He would have done the same. "I am assuming you want me to investigate him."

"Yes. I would do some querying myself, but with Lily feeling poorly most of the time, I would rather not be away from her. Also, if Emily knew I was snooping around behind her back, she would give me one of her tiresome dressing-downs. Frankly, I would prefer to avoid that nonsense altogether."

"I understand." Michael was gratified to discover he wasn't the only person always on the receiving end of her vitriol.

"She is quite hotheaded, as you know," Colin continued. "I daresay if she were a man, she would have engaged in a duel or two by now."

Michael hid a smile. She certainly was impetuous, a quality he found both intriguing and exasperating. As always though, he kept that information to himself.

"So, my friend . . . will you help me out?" Colin asked.

Michael took another drink of the port. "Of course."

"I will pay you for your time, naturally."

Holding up his hand, Michael shook his head. "Absolutely not. Consider this a favor for a friend." And a favor to himself. This was a prime opportunity for Michael to learn as much as he could about Pembrooke. Even though he knew he could never have Emily, he wanted to make sure that whoever she became involved with was a proper gentleman, one who would cherish her the way she deserved.

"I appreciate your assistance," Colin said. "It is at times like these I wish my father was alive, what with Diana engaged and Emily on the marriage-mart." He rubbed his forehead with the tips of his fingers. "I want to see them happily married to good men. But as we both know, one has to navigate these pre-marriage waters carefully."

"I wouldn't worry about it too much. I know you will do the right thing. Although"—Michael added with a smirk—"if you are this protective of your sisters and the babe Lily is carrying is a girl, I hate to think how you will be once your daughter comes of age."

"I have a list of convents at the ready," Colin quipped.

Michael chuckled. He always enjoyed the time he spent with his friend, away from the intrigues and stress of his job. It had become tiring to maintain his ruse for so many years, and he didn't know how much longer he could keep it up. Colin's mention of his father had dredged up memories of his own father, who had died when Michael was ten. Oftentimes he had wished for his wisdom and guidance, and lately he had felt the need more strongly than ever. Whenever he did have the urge to talk to someone honestly, he confided in his partner, Clewes, a seasoned spy who was a few years older than his father had been. The man had been as much of a father-figure to him over the years as anyone could be. But as much as he appreciated Clewes's direction and concern, it wasn't the same. No one could replace his father.

"You have become pensive all of the sudden," Colin observed. "Is anything wrong?"

"Sorry. Just have a bit on my mind as of late."

"About your future?"

Michael arched a brow in surprise. "What made you come to that conclusion?"

Colin leaned back in his chair and crossed his ankle over his knee. "Just some things I have observed over the past year. You seem to be restless, Michael. Lily has noticed it too."

"And I see you have honed your detection skills."

"I had a good teacher." He uncrossed his leg and leaned forward, looking at Michael intently. "What do you plan to do about your future, Michael? Have you made any decisions about it? Surely you do not think you can remain a spy forever."

Michael didn't reply right away. "There are no decisions to be made," he finally said. "My life is already set in stone. There is nothing I can do to change it."

"Do you really believe that?"

Rising from his chair, Michael walked to the fireplace. He stared at the portrait of Lily's parents, the Duke and Duchess of Breckenridge, hanging on the wall above the mantle. The painting was well done, capturing the great love the couple had for each other. It was a nice tribute to Colin's in-laws. "I will admit I have had doubts lately about how long I can continue with all of this. I wonder how much longer I can keep the deception up. Or if I even want to."

"Then why not resign? Twelve years of total devotion to England is sufficient enough. No one would dare say you didn't give your all for king and country."

"But if I did that, then what?" He faced Colin. "What would I do? Where would I go? I still cannot reveal what I have been all these years. To do so would put Mother in danger. I would have to leave London, and probably England."

Colin frowned. "I see your problem. You are worried there will be no one to care for the countess."

"No, that is not the issue. I have enough money to make sure she is protected and cared for the rest of her life."

"Then something else must be stopping you."

Michael turned back to the fireplace. The fire crackled and popped, filling the room with warmth. Even in June the temperatures tended to dip on cloudy days. A spark landed on his trousers, and he absently brushed it off.

He knew what was holding him back, what was keeping him from leaving London. It wasn't an overwhelming loyalty to the crown. It was the thought of seeing Emily on a very-limited basis, or possibly never seeing her again at all. He was hopeless, continuing to wish impossible things. Without thinking he pounded his fist against the mantel.

"Michael?"

"A thousand pardons. Forgot myself." He turned and gave Colin a half grin to cover his consternation. Handing his friend the empty glass, he said, "I will start my inquiries about Pembrooke immediately. We'll soon find out if he's up to anything shady."

Colin stood, giving him an odd look. When Michael didn't elaborate further, Colin shook his hand. "Thank you for your help regarding Pembrooke. I appreciate it."

"No problem." Michael straightened his cravat and smoothed his pomaded hair back into shape. He picked up his quizzing glass from the desk and polished the lens with the corner of his waistcoat. "When is the baby due?"

"Very soon. We are making plans to go to the country with Emily and Mother. William has been called into service for the war with America, and Diana wishes to stay in London with her friend, Helene. I think it is a good idea that she stay behind. While the rest of the family finds Leton House relaxing, it does tend to get boring for someone as social as Diana. Spending time with Helene will help her keep her mind off her fiancé."

"Sounds like a prime idea. I wish you a safe and happy journey. When will you return?"

"A couple months. Before the baby is born."

"Very well. I will see you when you get back." Michael walked toward the door. Before he turned the handle, Colin spoke.

"Michael."

Michael turned around and faced him.

"I am sure Pembrooke is a fine chap, and there is nothing to worry about. But just in case . . . be careful."

He grinned, genuinely this time, a smile borne of confidence. "No worries, Colin. I always am."

Colin and Lily's house wasn't too far from Michael's, and he relished the walk home. The afternoon air was brisk, but sunlight peeked in and out of the billowy clouds. He enjoyed walking, and tried to do it as often as possible. One could learn a lot by taking stock of his surroundings, which could be difficult to do while stuck inside a carriage.

Besides, he would have to pass Emily's house to get home. Somehow just being in somewhat close proximity to her was important to him.

As he strolled, he thought about his strategy to find out everything he could about Pembrooke. He would use Clewes as a resource, of course. The man could dig up the most pertinent of information at a moment's notice, and he would be highly discreet about it. Michael would also visit some of the gentlemen's clubs, such as White's. They were the primary gathering places of the men of the *ton,* where they could gather to drink, socialize, and of course, gamble. Without fail, the clubs had often provided him with a boon of knowledge.

As he reached Emily's house, a black carriage pulled up, labeled with unfamiliar markings. The driver jumped down and opened the door, and to Michael's surprise and consternation, Pembrooke exited from the vehicle. The man paused and looked at Michael for a moment, then tilted his hat in greeting, but didn't stop to exchange pleasantries. With light steps he strode up to the Dymoke's front door, knocked sharply, and entered once the Dymoke's butler, Blevins, opened the door.

Michael surmised that Colin would be none too pleased to see Pembrooke on his doorstep so soon to visit Emily. It had only been one day since the party. Michael wasn't thrilled with the prospect either. Colin had been correct, Pembrooke seemed serious about pursuing Emily. Michael's jaw clenched at the thought, but he had to shove his personal feelings aside. He had made a promise to Colin to help him find out more about Pembrooke. He never went back on his word. He had to deliver on it, and judging from Pembrooke's open eagerness, it would have to be soon. Michael hastened his steps, intent on putting his investigation in motion.

Chapter Five

Despite being caught off guard by Charles's sudden visit, Emily quite enjoyed having tea with him. Her mother seemed taken with him as well, and practically thrilled by the fact that she was actually entertaining someone. His manners were impeccable, a quality mothers always seemed to appreciate. He also said the right things at the right times. He even went so far to compliment Isabel's sandwiches, which were dry and tasteless, as usual. At the end of the light meal, Elizabeth even excused herself from the room for a few minutes, being mindful to leave the door open. Of course Charles, ever the gentleman, didn't take advantage of the freedom.

"Thank you for a delightful afternoon," Charles said a half hour later as he stood by the front door, putting on his hat. Blevins helped him into his lightweight coat.

"Thank you for coming by," Emily replied. "I had a nice time also." Which she did. It wasn't fantastic, but spending the afternoon with Charles had been a pleasant diversion.

Her words seemed to make him happy. He smiled. "Then may I extract the promise from you that we will do this again? In the near future?"

Emily's cheeks heated up at the way his gray eyes darkened to a smoky color as he looked at her. He was quite bold, actually. She hadn't been prepared for his request. He certainly knew how to keep her off balance. But it really didn't matter, since she couldn't see him again anyway. "I am sorry, but I do not think that will be possible."

His smile faded. "Why? Have I done something to offend you?"

"No, not at all," she said, quick to assuage him of the thought. "It is just that we won't be here, you see. Our family is leaving for Yorkshire at the end of the week, to our country home. We will be gone for the rest of the summer."

"I see." He cast his gaze to the hat in his hands, spun the brim around a few times, then looked up. "Would it be too forward of me to ask if I may see you in Yorkshire? To be honest with you, I do not think I can go an entire summer without visiting you again."

Well, now. That remark certainly had her eyebrows shooting up. He seemed most bent on seeing her as soon as possible, and she didn't know what to think about that. His eyes met hers in an intense gaze and her resolved drained as he continued to wait expectantly for her answer. "I suppose it would be all right," she finally agreed.

"Splendid!" Once again he gave her a beaming smile. It made him quite attractive, she had to admit. His black hair contrasted well with his fair skin, and he did have a strong profile, which she noticed as he turned toward the door. "Until next time, Miss Dymoke," he said, spinning around so he faced her again. He took her hand and planted a soft kiss on her knuckles. The move was so swift and seamless she didn't have time to react. He sped out the door, leaving her and Blevins alone in the foyer.

She stood for a moment, staring at the place on her hand his lips had touched. Once she regained her senses, she turned to the butler. The slender, proper man had been in their employ for years, and she trusted his judgment. If anyone could give her an honest answer it would be him. "What do you think of Mr. Pembrooke, Blevins?"

The butler appeared startled that she asked his opinion, but he quickly regained his composure. "He seems a nice enough chap, Miss Emily."

"Yes. He is nice." And attentive, and courteous, and all those other things she should be excited about. They were the same qualities Gavin had possessed. So why did she feel so unsettled? And not unsettled in a good way, like when she was head over toes for Gavin. It was more a sense of foreboding, that something wasn't quite right about the entire situation. Yet she couldn't put her finger on what it was.

Shrugging, she brushed off the negativity. She was merely guarding her heart, something she needed to do anyway. Gavin had hurt her once; she didn't want to experience that pain again. That had to be the reason for her uneasiness. There was no reason to make any more of it than that. "Thank you, Blevins. That will be all."

"You are most welcome, Miss Emily."

After Blevins left, she headed for the staircase. When she was halfway up the stairs, a sharp knock resounded on the door.

"I'll answer it," she said, turning around and walking to the entrance. Opening the door, her mouth fell open at the sight of Michael Balcarris, looking at her with a rather vivid expression through his quizzing glass.

"What, praytell, was Charles Pembroke doing here?"

Chapter Six

Emily frowned. Frankly, Michael's nosiness was starting to wear on her nerves. What right did he have to barge into her house and demand to know about her gentlemen callers? Actually, he pranced more than barged inside, but the result was the same. He was minding her business, and she didn't like it one bit, particularly since he hadn't expressed much interest in her suitors before.

As he glided by her and entered her home, she said, "Michael, please leave. You were not invited here."

"I will depart, dear Emily, once you tell me why you were entertaining Mr. Pembrooke." He turned and faced her, his expression bland. "You barely know the man."

"So? I know enough about him to see that he is a gentleman who knows how to conduct himself in the social graces—a quality you seem to lack in spades."

"I beg your pardon?" He peered at her through his quizzing glass, his eyes hooded and suddenly filled with defensive haughtiness.

"For the love of—would you just stop? Stop this . . . this nonsense!" She walked toward him until there were but a few inches between them. She had to look up, as the top of her head reached only his shoulders. "I am so tired of your ridiculousness." She searched his face, trying to find some remnant of the Michael she used to know. "Remember when we were children, Michael? Remember how much fun you used to be? How much fun you and Colin and I had together, once I was old enough to keep up with you? We used to laugh and play tricks on each other, and sit in the garden and tell funny stories until our insides hurt with laughter. Please tell me you haven't forgotten that, because I haven't."

Something flickered across his eyes, an indecipherable expression piercing the haughty boredom. For that instant she thought she actually saw the Michael Balcarris from her childhood. The one who used to star in her romantic dreams. The one who had affected her young heart like no one else had. But just as quickly, the brief moment disappeared.

"We were mere children at the time, Emily," he said snidely, still looking at her through the glass. "Adults are too old for such, ah, frivolity."

Frustration rose within her. Why couldn't she get through to him? "Frivolity? You, my dear sir, are the epitome of frivolity."

He shook his head slowly, as if he were speaking to a

dim-witted child. "Emily, Emily, Emily. Any *fun* we might have had together can merely be assigned to the fact that your brother and I were being kind to a pesky little girl."

Anger simmered beneath her surface. She bit the inside of her cheek in attempt to hold her tongue, but she couldn't maintain her composure for long. "You are the most frustrating, irritating, exasperating—"

"I see you have been working on your vocabulary," he interjected blandly.

"—*fop* I know. And even if it were one miniscule bit of your business why I had Mr. Pembrooke over for tea, I would not tell you."

"Emily!"

Both of them turned around to see Elizabeth Dymoke dashing into the foyer. "Who in the world are you arguing with?" She stopped up short when her gaze landed on Michael. Her face curled into a scowl. "What are *you* doing here?" she asked in a toxic tone.

"Leaving," Emily said. Her hands fisted at her sides. "He was just leaving. Right, Michael?"

He paused for a moment, then nodded, still managing to look completely unruffled. "I suppose I shall. I can see that I am not welcome here."

"No, you are not," Elizabeth said firmly. "Now, kindly take your leave, or I will ring for Blevins to escort you out."

He bowed deeply, appearing not to be offended in the least that two women were shooting verbal and visual daggers at him. "Cheerio," he said brightly, then spun with a flourish on his high, square heel and went out the door.

After he left, Emily took a deep breath. Her mother came over to her, placing an arm around her daughter's shoulders. "He upset you, didn't he? What did that cretin of a man say?"

"He was simply being his usual irritating self," Emily said, not wanting to discuss Michael's intrusion any further.

Exasperation crossed Elizabeth's features. "I shall have to speak to Ruby about her son," she said as they both walked out of the room and headed up the stairs. "I do not want him upsetting you anymore."

It was too late for that. She was already upset. However, Emily couldn't blame him completely. She really needed to learn to keep her emotions under control and not let him crawl under her skin every time they were around each other. "I don't think it would be necessary, Mama. I seriously doubt he will come round again."

Elizabeth cast her a dubious look, then relented. "Very well, I will not say anything to her. Poor Ruby," she added as they reached the top of the staircase. "I cannot fathom how a lovely woman like her could spawn such a wretched man."

Emily had to marvel at the irony of her mother's words. Up until last year, Elizabeth's opinion of Michael had been much different. She had even entertained a match between her daughter and Michael, a suggestion that had nearly gave Emily heart failure. But something had happened between Michael and her mother, an incident Elizabeth had never elaborated on. Emily knew better than to press her about it. Usually her mother was open with her thoughts and emotions, but when she remained tight-lipped about something it was best for everyone not to pry. But ever since the mysterious incident, Elizabeth had struggled to be civil to him, almost as much as Emily did.

"You should put that ridiculous man out of your mind at once, dear," Elizabeth said. "Why don't you join me in my sitting room? I am stitching a new piece of embroidery. Would you like to take a look at it?"

"Perhaps another time, Mother." Emily kissed her cheek. "I am a bit tired right now. I think I will catch up on some reading, then retire for the night."

"Well then. Enjoy yourself, darling," Elizabeth said. She kissed Emily's cheek. Then she paused. "Before you go, I would like to ask you something."

"Yes?"

"What do you think of Mr. Pembrooke?"

Emily hesitated for a brief moment before answering. "To be honest, Mama, I do not know what to think. He seems like a nice man."

"And quite handsome," Elizabeth added with a sly smile.

"Yes, that he is. But I still do not know him well enough to form an opinion."

"He does seem rather smitten with you."

Emily nodded, but couldn't admit to her mother that she found it hard to believe Charles had become so taken with her in such a short period of time.

"Of course, I'm not the least bit surprised," Elizabeth said.

"At least one of us isn't," Emily mumbled.

"Oh, darling." Elizabeth touched her daughter's cheek. "Do not doubt yourself so. You are a beautiful young woman with a fiery spirit. I know you have had a hard time dealing with Gavin's departure."

Emily sucked in a breath. "I did not know you knew about that," she said.

"About your feelings for him? Dearest, you would be surprised what a mother knows." She grasped Emily's hand and squeezed it tightly. "Gavin is a nice enough man, and he was right to let you go, considering his feelings for Diana. You have to let him go as well."

Emily's head was spinning. How could her mother have known all this and not said a word? She had thought the woman had been completely in the dark about the whole situation with Gavin. "I am working on that," she said, but didn't elaborate. While she loved her mother dearly and they shared a closeness, for some reason she didn't feel like she could discuss this with her.

"That's good, darling. Forget about Charles, and put that loathsome Michael Balcarris out of your mind as well. And always remember, I am here if you need me." She released her hand and patted the back of it. "Good night."

"Thank you, Mama," she said, giving her a smile. "Good night."

Emily entered her bedroom and shut the door. Slipping off her shoes, she did as her mother suggested and turned her thoughts away from Gavin and Michael and even off of Charles. She sat down on her bed and picked up the local gossip sheet from her nightstand. Soon she was engrossed in reading the paper, catching up on the comings and goings of the citizens of London and the local news and scandals making their rounds in society. She even managed to forget about the three men altogether. An hour later she grew sleepy and decided to go to bed.

But when she lay down and snuggled with Bronwyn, her tabby cat, it wasn't the latest society tittle-tattle or Gavin or even Charles that entered her mind.

For some indecipherable reason, it was Michael.

Michael's pride stung as he made his way down the Dymoke's sidewalk and turned to head toward his flat. He had been on Emily's most-hated list for a long time, but had only recently been added to her mother's. The memory of his conversation with Elizabeth last year penetrated his thoughts, a conversation he had tried to forget. To dissuade her matchmaking intentions, he had insulted Emily's figure and her personage with enough malice he had been surprised Elizabeth hadn't challenged him to a duel to defend her honor. Every syllable he'd expelled from his mouth was false, but he had said the derogatory words with such sincerity her mother believed that *he* believed it. Thus was the end of her matchmaking and the beginning of her loathing.

Yet another price to pay for the isolating life he'd chosen.

He walked home briskly, planning to meet with Clewes and discuss Pembrooke. Time was of the essence because of Pembrooke's fervent interest in Emily. He tried to put her out of his mind. He was at the breaking point of being on the end of her vitriolic tirades, even if he didn't blame her too much for it. If he had to deal with someone of similar personality as his alter ego, he wouldn't suffer him gladly either. Although he had to admit that lately Emily was acting more and more like a spoiled brat whenever they were around each other. They hadn't had a civil conversation between them in at least a year.

The less he thought about Emily, the better. He needed to focus on the matter at hand—Charles Pembrooke. He would busy himself with that task, and honor Emily's wishes by staying away from her. This way they would both manage to maintain their distance—and their sanity.

Chapter Seven

"Thank you so much for coming over and helping me pack," Lily said, folding one of her petticoats into a neat square. "Colin wanted to help, but I told him no. He has been difficult to be around as of late."

"Will you be taking this, my lady?" Hannah, Lily's maid, interrupted. She held up a cream-colored formal evening gown studded with tiny seed pearls.

"I doubt it fits anymore, so I do not think I will," Lily replied, touching her slightly swelled belly. "Hannah, Emily and I can finish up here. Why don't you see if Francoise needs help in the kitchen?"

"Yes, my lady." Hannah made a hasty exit out of the room.

Lily looked at Emily and smiled. "Now we can speak freely."

Emily carefully placed another one of Lily's plumed

hats in its box. They were preparing for the family's trip to their country house in Yorkshire. Emily had already packed her suitcases and was eager to be on her way. She adored the country, and couldn't wait to get out of the stifling confines of the city.

"Is my brother nervous about the baby?" she asked, fastening the hat box closed.

"Absolutely. I tell him there is nothing to be concerned about, but he continues to fuss over me as if I might shatter at any moment."

Emily looked at her. "I fail to see what you're complaining about. It sounds like he adores you."

Lily blushed. "I am quite lucky, aren't I? He is the most wonderful man, you know." She moved toward Emily, displaying a slight waddle to her gait. Lily was tall and thin, physical characteristics that had been quite a cross to bear in a society that valued petite stature. She had struggled with feelings of insecurity and self-consciousness for years. However, Lily was lovely in her own way, with hair the color of chestnuts and large round eyes to match. When she had married Colin, who was considered one of the most handsome men in London, she had turned a few heads as well as raised a few eyebrows. No one had expected him to wed a woman who wasn't considered his physical equal. Yet Colin hadn't cared one whit what anyone else had thought and had married for love. Many of society's most eligible bachelorettes had mourned their marriage.

Emily glanced at Lily. Unlike many pregnant women who often gained weight in their faces and hips, the only signs she was with child were the small mound barely visible beneath her dress and her glowing countenance. She seemed beyond happy. Marriage and pregnancy definitely suited her.

The two women had become friends nearly three years ago, when Emily had debuted at court for the first time. A short time later, Lily had met Colin, and after a brief courtship, had announced their engagement. Emily had been thrilled to have her best friend become her sister-in-law. But soon after the wedding, time with Lily had been scarce. Emily understood, after all Lily had her duties as the wife of a baron and a new household to run. But Emily couldn't help but miss the talks she and her friend used to have.

"There is something bothering you." Lily laid a hand on Emily's arm. "I can tell. I know we have not had the chance to talk as much as we used to, and I miss that. But you know I am always here for you."

"I know you are, and I appreciate it. You know how much I treasure our friendship."

"Then let me help."

Emily looked away. "It is nothing, Lily, really. I am merely missing Gavin, that is all."

"Oh, Emily." Lily ducked her head, trying to meet her friend's gaze. "When I heard he left the country, I knew you would have a hard time with it. But when I saw you dancing with that man the other night at the Balcarris's, I thought maybe you had moved on."

Emily sighed. "I am trying, Lily. Truly I am. And sometimes I feel like I have. Then other times I cannot stop thinking about him. I cannot just unlove him now, can I?"

"Perhaps not. But I know you will find someone else you'll love even more. Someone who will love you with the passion and depth you deserve."

"Funny," Emily said bitterly. "Gavin basically said the same thing." She flopped down on the one empty space amid the many items of clothing on Lily and Colin's bed and smoothed out a small patch of the brocaded bedspread. "To be honest, Gavin is not the only thing on my mind as of late."

"Oh?" Lily sat on a small settee near the window, directly across from the bed. "What else has been troubling you?"

"Michael Balcarris, for starters."

Lily let out a long-suffering sigh. "I do not understand why you let him get to you so much. He is quite a harmless man."

"*Man* isn't exactly the word I would use to describe him."

"Emily," Lily said, using the tone she often reserved when Emily teetered on the fine line between witty banter and tasteless insults, something that she did fairly often where Michael was concerned.

"Sorry," Emily mumbled, not sounding the least bit contrite. "But I wish he wasn't so blasted nosy. Or so blasted *present*. Every time I turn around, whether I am at a party or the opera or even in Hyde Park, he is there."

"Now that is not true. There are periods where Michael is abroad for lengths of time. You know that."

"The respites from his insufferable presence are not nearly long enough, I am afraid."

A smile twitched on Lily's lips. "Let's not talk about Michael. The topic never fails to bring you to near apoplexy. What about the chap you were dancing with the other night?"

"Charles?"

"Is that his name? I have never seen him before, and Colin couldn't place him either."

"He is new to London. A long lost relative of Lord Mumblethorpe. Twice removed, I believe."

Lily's brows arched. "He is rather prime-looking, don't you think?"

For the first time that afternoon, Emily smiled. "Why yes, my scheming friend, he is quite prime indeed. And he has already come to the house for tea."

"Really? And it has taken you this long to tell me such an important detail?" Lily pretended to pout, a tactic she undoubtedly used on Colin. Knowing her brother's absolute devotion to his wife, Emily surmised he had probably fallen for it a time or two. "What kind of friend, no, what kind of sister-in-law makes some-one drag that sort of information out of her?"

"It didn't seem important." Emily shrugged.

"Emily, you well know that when a gentleman calls on a lady, he is showing interest in pursuing her. Stop being coy."

"Fine. He came, we had tea, Mama thinks he hung the moon and the stars, and he wants to see me again. Is that enough detail for you?"

"It will do," Lily said with a wide grin. "For now. Except I need to know one more thing."

Emily got up from the bed. "What?"

"Do you want to see him again?"

She hesitated. "Frankly, I am not sure what I want. If I am interested in Charles, it seems like I am being disloyal to Gavin, as preposterous as that sounds."

"Not as preposterous as you think," Lily murmured.

"At any rate, I should be welcoming this kind of attention. As you so astutely said a few minutes ago, I should find someone to love me."

Lily shook her head. "I did not *exactly* say it that way."

"But the meaning is clear. And deep down, I do know that I need to move on. So, why not do so with Charles? He's handsome, charming, and pleasant enough."

"But?"

"But . . ." Emily threaded her fingers together. "There is something missing. I don't know what it is. Maybe we just need to know each other better."

"Well, that is a given, considering you barely know each other at all."

Emily moved closer to Lily. "How long did it take for you to fall in love with Colin?"

"About five minutes."

"Seriously."

"Not much longer. Maybe a week, or two. I think he was a little slower to come round. It took him about three."

"Sounds like my brother. He can be a little daft sometimes."

"We all can, Emily. Especially when it comes to love. It makes us do stupid and irrational things. But it also warms our hearts, bodies and souls. Maybe Charles is the man to warm your heart and soul, maybe he isn't."

"But how will I know? I thought Gavin was the one. You see how wrong I was about him."

Lily rose from the settee. "Listen to your heart. Let it guide you. It will lead you to the truth."

As the women continued to pack, Emily pondered Lily's words. They were wise, and she would do well to heed them. Lily's heart had led her to Colin, and they were by far the most happily married couple she knew. However, she had listened to her heart regarding Gavin, and that ended in an embarrassing disaster. Before that, she had actually entertained romantic notions about Michael. At least she could blame her age on that one. But she had no excuse where Gavin was concerned.

Emily wondered if she could ever trust her heart again.

Michael took a small sip of brandy and sank back in the leather chair. He had been nursing his drink for the past hour, as sobriety was a necessity when discreetly observing others. He surveyed the scene at White's. The regulars here often spent hours and hours drinking and gambling, many times losing most if not all their fortunes. Yet it was one of the best places in the city to find out information, so he continued to patronize the club. Usually it was teeming with gentlemen, however, tonight the crowd was light and only a few members were present. Some were seated at various tables around the room, engaged in conversation or in games of chance. But despite the low turnout, drink flowed freely while cigar and cheroot smoke blanketed the air.

Michael didn't expect to learn much tonight. In fact, his investigation of Pembrooke had come to a quick and frustrating dead end. So far he and Clewes had turned up nothing. Even with the assistance of Clewes's newest protégé, Barnes, the men had failed to uncover anything out of the ordinary regarding the man. Even his story about being a relative of Mumblethorpe's had panned out. Strange indeed, since Michael could have sworn Mumblethorpe hadn't a single male cousin.

On the bright side, Colin would rest easy when he found out his sister's suitor was above reproach. Michael couldn't say the same for himself. Despite knowing that Emily would eventually marry, the possibility of it being on the horizon was like a stab in the heart.

He sipped his drink again. The smoke surrounding him permeated everything. Personally he abhorred that habit. Then he caught a whiff of the sweet aroma of a pipe. Now, that was a different story. His father, Timothy, had smoked one, and Michael still held memories of climbing into the earl's lap at the tender age of six, listening to stories of his travels throughout the world as cherry-scented smoke wafted around them. The senior Earl of Hathery had been an adventurer, and while he had loved his wife and son, wanderlust was never far from his heart. During a trip to Spain he had caught cholera and died when Michael was eight. Michael assumed he had inherited his father's sense of adventure and intrigue. But unlike how his father had felt, as of late the thought of staying home seemed more and more appealing.

"May I join you?"

Michael glanced up. Speak of the devil. Charles Pembrooke stood in front of him, a small glass of port in his hand. He gestured to the chair next to Michael. "If you are waiting for someone, I apologize for disturbing you."

Michael tilted his chin and hooded his eyes. This opportunity had landed in his lap, but he would still keep up his guard. "No, I am alone. You may join me if you, ah, prefer."

"Splendid." Charles sat down and crossed one leg over the other. "Lord Mumblethorpe recommended this club to me. It is a prime place, just as he said. I can see the appeal."

"I suppose."

Charles set his drink down on the small round table in between the two chairs. "Do you mind if I ask you a question?"

Michael nodded slowly, but kept his gaze on the rest of the room.

"How close are you to Emily Dymoke?"

Gripping his drink more tightly, Michael turned and faced him, fighting to maintain his façade of apathy. "What an odd question. Why do you ask?"

"Merely curious, as I saw you outside her home the other day. And on the balcony with her the night we first met. She insists that you and she are just friends."

He had a hard time believing Emily had said anything

of the sort. Possibly she admitted they were acquaintances, although stating they were utter enemies was more likely. He wasn't about to say that to Pembrooke, however. "I fail to see how my relationship with, ah, Miss Dymoke, is any business of yours."

Charles held up his hands in his defense. "I meant no offense, Lord Hathery. I simply want to make sure that, by courting her, I would not be entering into a competition for her affections."

Michael's heart compressed. So Pembrooke did have designs on Emily, and had just declared his intentions toward her. He wanted nothing more than to grab the man by the collar and tell him in no uncertain terms that Emily was off limits. But he couldn't. He couldn't say anything of the sort. He didn't have the right to do so.

Instead, he slowly sipped his brandy, then said, "I have known Miss Dymoke since we were children. The idea of the two of us as anything but friends can only be considered, if you will pardon my crassness, practically incestuous."

Pembrooke leaned back in his chair, relief crossing his features. "That is good to hear. Surely you understand, I had to ask. She is a lovely young woman, and frankly I am surprised she has not married already."

"She has discerning taste." He didn't add that her taste had dropped considerably if she was interested in Pembrooke.

"Well, I hope I meet her high standards." Pembrooke drained his port in one gulp. "It's been a pleasure, Lord

Hathery, but I must be off. Tea is in an hour, and Lord Mumblethorpe expects punctuality. Cheerio."

Arching a brow in return, Michael remained silent as he projected boredom, not wanting to tip his hand. He watched Pembrooke leave White's, pausing by Cavendish, one of the attendants. Pembrooke waited while the attendant went to retrieve his hat and coat.

Michael stood nonchalantly and left his half-empty glass on the table near his chair. Making sure he wasn't observed by Pembrooke, he inched closer until he was within earshot, picking up the two men's voices in mid-conversation.

"The Dymoke's usually leave for Yorkshire about this time, Mr. Pembrooke," Cavendish said as he handed the younger man his hat. "Why do you ask?"

"Lord Mumblethorpe had mentioned something to me about Miss Emily heading for the country. I thought I would make some inquiries to determine more specifics."

Michael's eyes narrowed slightly. Pembrooke had just made his first misstep. Mumblethorpe and the Dymoke's ran in completely different circles. They might attend the same parties occasionally, but the family would hardly divulge anything more personal to the addled man than the fact that he preferred dappled horses to chestnut ones. Now Michael was assured Pembrooke was up to something. He vowed to find out exactly what as he paid deeper attention to their discussion.

Cavendish nodded as his face split into a grin. Unlike most attendants, the man talked more than he listened.

"So it's Miss Emily you are interested in, eh? That is a switch. Usually Miss Diana gets all the attention."

"Yes, it is a shame Miss Diana is already spoken for, as she will undoubtedly have the biggest dowry."

"So it is marriage that you are after, then?"

"Absolutely." Pembrooke put on his hat. "I believe our marriage will greatly benefit both of us." He lowered his voice. "Sometimes a man finds himself in a precarious financial position, if you know what I mean."

Cavendish's expression filled with sympathy. "Yes, Mr. Pembrooke. Unfortunately I do. Therefore, I wish you luck in your quest for the young lady's hand." He handed Pembrooke his coat. "Have a good evening, sir."

"Thank you, Cavendish. I plan to."

Michael clenched his fists. Now Pembrooke's true intentions were out in the open, although he wondered at Pembrooke's cavalier attitude in divulging such personal information to someone like Cavendish. But he dwelled more on Pembrooke's message than its delivery. He would marry Emily solely for her money, and no other reason. Not only that, but it wouldn't be a stretch of the imagination to imply that Pembrooke would eventually drag Emily into another "precarious financial position" once he drained her coffers. Michael couldn't allow that to happen.

He stopped to get his hat, then double backed to find Asquith, the man in charge of dispensing the drinks. Michael found him in the corner of the club, polishing one of the empty mahogany tables.

"Good evening, Lord Hathery," Asquith said, thrusting the rag in his pocket. He ran a quick hand over his thinning blond hair, smoothing down the two frizzy strands that swooped over the top of his head. "What can I do for you this evening?"

Reaching in his pocket, Michael took out his money clip. "A friend of mine had to leave," he said, peeling off a couple of the bills. "I wanted to pay his tab." He also wanted to find out exactly how much Pembrooke owed the establishment. It wouldn't give him a complete picture of how dire Pembrooke's financial straits were, but it was a start.

"What is your friend's name?"

"Charles Pembrooke."

"Ah, yes. Mr. Pembrooke. A nice young fellow. I believe he's only been here twice. I understand he is new to London?"

"Yes." Michael didn't offer any more information.

"Well, you do not have to bother with his tab. He is paid in full."

"He is?"

"He also gave a generous tip. As I said, a very nice fellow."

Odd. If Pembrooke was having trouble with money, it would be expected that he would have a tab of some sort. Although some men who were in debt past their eyebrows often desperately overspent money, rarely did they pay their bills on time, especially small ones. That is, unless they had suddenly become flush with blunt.

Michael suspected Pembrooke was so certain Emily would agree to his proposal that he already started borrowing against her dowry.

Pembrooke's outrageous confidence only made Michael more determined to keep him and Emily apart. And he knew exactly how he could do just that.

Chapter Eight

"You want me to go to Yorkshire? To visit Elizabeth?" Ruby Balcarris, Countess Hathery and Michael's devoted mother, put down the linen handkerchief she had been monogramming with a large, red letter B and looked at her son. "I do not know, darling. Do you not think it would be terribly rude to arrive unannounced?"

"For anyone else, yes. But Elizabeth is one of your dearest friends. I seriously doubt she would object to you visiting her at Leton House."

Ruby touched her fingertip to her lips. "Perhaps not. And I will admit it would be good to get out of the city this summer. It can be rather odiferous, to put it mildly. Oh, it has been ages since I have visited the country."

Guilt nagged at him as her enthusiasm grew. His mother had never once stated to him that she wanted to leave London. Their own country estate in the Dales had been abandoned for years, ever since his father had passed away. He had assumed that she had no interest in going back. "If you had wanted to depart London, Mother, all you had to do was tell me. We could have gone to the country together long before this."

"Oh, Michael, you are so busy with . . . well, with whatever it is that occupies your time. I did not want to bother you. Besides, you know how much I love my home here. However, I believe you are right. It is high time that I venture outside the city. And of course I adore spending time with Elizabeth." Suddenly a shadow passed across Ruby's eyes as she averted her gaze for a moment.

"Mother?" Michael asked, concern tingeing his tone.

She looked at him again. "Are you not worried with how Elizabeth might receive you? She has not held you in high regard ever since that unfortunate incident between the two of you. Although I do feel she is being rather irrational about the whole thing. There is such a thing as forgiveness, you know."

Michael looked away. He didn't particularly relish that Emily's mother held him in such minimal esteem.

"I tried to reason with her, to tell her that you really did not mean all those horrible things you said about Emily last year." She eyed him guardedly. "You did not mean them, did you? I have to confess I found your words extremely harsh toward young Emily. It was almost as if you had some sort of grudge against her."

He pretended to brush an imaginary piece of fluff off his shoulder while he gathered his thoughts. Lying to

Emily on a regular basis was painful enough, fibbing to his mother just added to his discomfort. Not to mention that she clearly had her doubts about his character as well. "Mother, I wanted Lady Dymoke to understand that I am not interested in Emily. She is merely a friend. Nothing more. The sole purpose of my remarks to Lady Dymoke were to add emphasis to the obvious fact that her daughter and I are most ill-suited."

"But why do you think that? She is a perfectly lovely girl. Smart, charming, witty, really everything a man could want in a wife." Ruby twisted the emerald ring on her finger. Michael's father had given it to her the year before he died. It was a habit she indulged when she became anxious.

Michael's shoulders tensed. "Is there something wrong, Mother?"

"I have been putting off discussing this with you, but I suppose I cannot avoid the subject forever."

Michael sat down on the dainty chaise in his mother's sitting room. The furniture in the room always seemed at least two sizes too small. He steeled himself. The conversation had taken an unusual, yet eventual, turn. He knew what she wanted to discuss. He couldn't have expected her to not ever question his unusual lifestyle and behavior.

"You know I love you, darling," she said softly, finally glancing up at him. "Although I will admit that during the past ten years or so, your—how shall I put it—demeanor, has puzzled me. You are not the same person who left for Oxford."

"People change, Mother."

"Yes, but your changes have been so . . . unusual." She waved her hand as if discussing this particular topic was distasteful to her. "Never mind that. That is not what I wanted to chat with you about. To be honest, what I am really concerned about is the future of our family. You and I are the only ones left. It is up to you to carry on the Hathery earldom."

At his mother's words, Emily's image wafted across his mind. He pushed it away and stood from the chaise. "There is plenty of time for that. Thirty is not so very old."

"Your father died at thirty."

His heart softened toward her. He reached out and touched her cheek. "But I am still here. And I will be here for a long time." He patted her face. "So do not fret, Mother. I am fine and quite content with my lot in life. You should concentrate on having a splendid time with the Dymokes."

Ruby placed her hand over Michael's. "Thank you, dear. But promise me one thing."

"Anything, Mother."

"You will think about what I said? Please, take it seriously. Consider finding a wife and having a family. We cannot let the Hathery name die out."

It took everything he had not to draw her into his arms, to reassure her that everything would be all right. But he didn't, not when he couldn't make her any promises. "I will," was all he could say.

"Thank you. Now, to change the subject, when do you want to leave for Yorkshire?"

"Tomorrow, after breakfast. The Dymoke's left a few hours ago, and they always stop at the Raven's Wing Inn on the way. We should arrive the day after they do."

"Then I better go pack," Ruby said, smiling as she left the room.

Michael could see his mother was excited about the trip, and another pang of guilt prodded him. Once he took care of the problem with Pembrooke, he would make sure his mother thoroughly enjoyed her holiday.

He left the drawing room and headed for his bedroom to pack his things for the trip north. Once he had everything prepared, he went to Clewes's quarters. He needed to give him final instructions before leaving in the morning.

Clewes had already retired for the evening, but when he answered the door, the older gentleman didn't seem to mind being disturbed. Michael informed him about his impromptu visit to Yorkshire.

"I have left everything in good order, Clewes. I should be back no later than a fortnight. If there is any communication from the crown, please forward it to me immediately."

"Yes, my lord."

"Thank you, as always, for your assistance. We will be off early in the morn. Is there anything you need before we go?"

Clewes paused. "My lord," he said in a grave tone. "May I have a word?"

"Of course." The seriousness of Clewes demeanor tripped a wire of concern in Michael.

"Please, come in," Clewes said, holding the door open wider.

As he walked into Clewes room, it dawned on Michael that he'd never been in the man's quarters before. Up until that point, Clewes had exclusively sought Michael out, thus eliminating any need for Michael to view Clewes's room.

Clewes had lived—contentedly, Michael had assumed—in an unoccupied area of the Balcarris home. On the infrequent occasions Ruby had seen Clewes, she had concluded he was Michael's valet. The man kept his abode as sparse as a valet's—a small bed in the corner covered with a simple spread. A petite armoire in the opposite corner. Simple shaving stand near the armoire. Next to that laid an old chest that had traversed possibly every continent. The meagerness of his living conditions didn't surprise Michael in the least. The man was concise in every facet of his life.

Clewes's request to speak with him in the privacy of his chambers, however, did surprise him, in addition to raising hackles of concern.

"I have something of great import to discuss with you, my lord." Clewes set down the candlestick on the shaving stand, then turned and faced Michael. "I am afraid I will no longer be able to continue my partnership with you. I am leaving for France day after tomorrow."

Typical Clewes. Blunt. Direct. To the point. And completely knocking Michael off-kilter.

"Understandably, this must come as quite a shock," Clewes said matter-of factly.

"That would be an understatement. I never thought I would hear you say those words to me, Clewes." Michael had always assumed the man would remain his partner until . . . well, he hadn't actually thought about their partnership ever ending.

"To be honest, my lord, I never thought to say them. Not while you were still in service to England. However, there has been a development that needs my urgent attention."

Michael crossed his arms. It was a petulant gesture, but he was feeling petulant at the moment. How could he function without Clewes? The man had been his right hand for the past twelve years. His mentorship was invaluable. To continue with his work without him seemed unfathomable. "I cannot imagine any type of development that would require you to sever our relationship."

"It is not a severance, exactly." For the first time in Michael's recollection, Clewes seemed a tad less sure of himself. "And I would hope that no matter how many miles separate us, our friendship will always endure. You must know how difficult it is for me to say this to you, to leave you and England behind."

"Then why must you leave at all? What could possibly be there for you in France?"

"Marguerite."

A woman? Michael arched a brow. Clewes had never mentioned being involved with anyone. In fact, Michael had taken it for granted that the man chose to live like a monk, just as Michael had, because it was the easiest course of action, at least where the job was concerned.

Personally, it was a living hell.

Still, Michael could hardly comprehend that one woman would cause Clewes to give up the profession he had devoted his life to. "Is she in danger?" he asked, his mind spinning with possible scenarios.

"No. But, she is running out of patience. With me." Clewes paused, inhaled a deep breath, then continued. "We met nearly twenty years ago. She was young, beautiful, and for some incomprehensible reason, she fell in love with me. Naturally, I loved her to distraction. Yet I was bound to my duty, and I could not give that up. She said she understood, and we have tried to make a go of it all these years. However, correspondence and infrequent clandestine visits to France are not enough for her anymore. Obviously I can hardly blame her."

"So you are giving up spying to be with her."

Clewes nodded. "It is not a decision I take lightly, let me assure you. But once I came to the conclusion, I knew I had made the right one. I do not have that many years left, my lord. I want to spend the rest of them being happy with Marguerite."

Michael uncrossed his arms. The man had made up his mind, and there was nothing Michael could do or say to change it. "Again, Clewes, you never fail to surprise me. However, it is clear that you are content with your decision. I suppose there is nothing I can do but accept it."

Clewes lips formed into a rarely seen smile. "Marguerite is a strong woman, and she has supported me for nearly two decades. I have been more than unfair to her during that time. I no longer want her to put her life on hold on my account."

"Of course you wouldn't." Michael stepped forward and extended his hand in a gesture of congratulations, setting aside his own selfish response to feel genuine joy for his mentor. "I am happy for you then, my friend, and I wish you well."

Clewes shook Michael's hand with enthusiasm, allowing a sliver of his elation to show. Just as quickly, though, his expression reverted to its earlier seriousness. "If I may offer you a bit of advice, my lord. Do not make the same mistake I made."

Michael stiffened as he let go of Clewes's hand. "What do you mean?" he asked, although he suspected he already knew what Clewes was referring to.

"Miss Dymoke. You love her."

"No, I—"

"Do not try to deny it, my lord. I understand. I was in your position so many years ago. But instead of acknowledging my feelings, I denied them. Fortunately, Marguerite is a patient woman. But I fear Miss Dymoke does not possess such infinite endurance. If you let her go, you risk spending your life alone."

Michael averted his gaze. He wouldn't question how

Clewes had uncovered his secret. He merely accepted it. "She deserves better than me," he said.

"I thought Marguerite did too. But she did not agree."

"I do not think you can compare Emily and I with you and Marguerite. There is one important component missing. Marguerite loves you. Emily reviles me. She is not even mine to let go."

"I am certain that is because she does not know you, my lord. The real you, that is." Clewes cleared his throat. "Let me ask you this. Is she worth anything to you?"

Scowling, Michael said, "You know she is. What is your point?"

"My point is, is she worth enough for you to give it all up? The danger, the intrigue, the adventure?"

"It is not that simple and you know it."

"Forgive me, my lord, but it is. We are the ones who make it complicated. There will always be young men keen to join our ranks. Edward Barnes is a good example."

Michael thought about the fresh-faced young man Clewes had been training. He was as eager a pupil as Michael had ever seen, and would make an excellent agent.

"Do not think yourself indispensable," Clewes continued. "Especially not at the expense of your happiness, or the happiness of someone you love. That is a choice you will live to regret."

"I *am* happy, Clewes. This is the life I chose for myself. It is satisfying."

"Oh yes. It satisfies your pride. Your inquisitive nature. Your loyalty to the crown. But does it satisfy your soul? Does it fill the emptiness in your heart?"

Michael regarded his mentor. It seemed more than odd to be discussing matters of the heart with him, yet Michael knew he couldn't have this conversation with anyone else. No one other than Clewes would understand the personal sacrifice Michael had made over the years. Which made him take Clewes words as seriously as possible.

"You do not have to decide anything right now, my lord. I just ask that you think about the matter further."

"I will," Michael promised solemnly. It suddenly dawned on him that within the span of a day he had been told to ponder his future marriage prospect by two people who meant the world to him. Ironically, neither of them truly knew how much he cherished them both.

"I do leave you with a word of caution, my lord," Clewes said, his tone grave. Do not wait too long to decide what to do. You do not want to let Miss Dymoke slip through your fingers. For if you do . . . you will never get her back."

Chapter Nine

Emily's head felt as if it would bounce right off her neck. The road to Yorkshire had been plagued with dips, ruts, and holes the entire journey. Her whole body ached from being jostled and tossed about, and more than once she'd accidentally bumped into the side of the carriage. Across from her sat her mother, who for some inexplicable reason could actually sleep through the tumultuous ride. Emily had even heard her light snoring a time or two as they traversed the few smooth stretches of road.

She could only imagine how Lily was managing in the other carriage. Certainly the bumpy journey had taken its toll on the expectant woman. Knowing how overprotective Colin had been throughout the pregnancy so far, she figured he was probably yelling useless instructions at their poor driver.

Fortunately, after thirty more minutes of body-raising travel, the coach came to a welcome stop. Emily peeked outside the black curtain at the lush greenery before her. This was their usual luncheon stopping place, where they set out a lovely picnic near the side of the road, and replenished their water supply from the cool, clear stream nearby. Her stomach suddenly growled. She hadn't realized she was hungry until that moment. Usually she was acutely aware of her appetite.

"Are we there yet?" Elizabeth mumbled, coming out of her sleep.

"We are stopping for lunch."

The door to the coach opened, and their new driver, Edmond, held out his hand. Colin had hired him only yesterday, as their usual driver was navigating his personal vehicle. He looked a tiny bit older than Emily, with dark brown hair and a bushy beard and mustache. "M'lady," he said, extending his hand to Elizabeth. She took it and stepped out of the carriage. He did the same for Emily. The two women didn't travel with a maid, as Leton House had its own servants, including Estelle, the cook, and Olive, the maid of all work.

"Your food will be ready in a wink," Edmond said. He then left to meet up with Hannah, Lily's maid, from Colin's coach. As the daughter of a duke and the wife of a baron, Lily was always accompanied by her own assistant. It was especially necessary now because of the pregnancy. Emily surmised Colin probably appreciated the extra help.

She inhaled the fresh, earthy aroma of the air. It was

so different from London, and so inviting. Her mind and soul settled immediately and the aches in her body from the trip disappeared. There was something about the verdant landscape surrounding her that brought her peace and put her at ease. She took in the leafy trees, thick grass, and stems of colorful wildflowers. She couldn't help but smile as birds twittered all about her, their sweet songs filtering through her ears.

How she loved the country. She couldn't wait to get to Leton House and saddle her horse, Chandler, a dappled gray she'd had since he was a colt. She didn't do much riding in London, simply because she hated the confines of the city. But she made up for it during the summer months, where she could ride her horse for hours across the countryside.

Within thirty minutes Hannah and Edmond had set out a lovely spread. Several varieties of cheeses, biscuits, cold meat pies, fresh strawberries and cream—it all made her mouth water. She lowered herself to the ground and tucked her skirts underneath her legs. Hannah handed her a pocket pie stuffed to bursting with tender beef.

Her mother joined her. Only Colin and Lily were missing.

"I wonder what is keeping them?" Elizabeth asked a few moments later, holding a small piece of yellow cheese between two delicate fingers.

"Well, Mama, technically they are still newly married," Emily said, grinning. "Perhaps they are reveling in their privacy."

"Emily!" Elizabeth scolded. "A lady doesn't speak of those things, especially in public. And most especially considering Lily's condition." Yet despite her reprimand, the corners of her lips twitched. She quickly popped the piece of cheese in her mouth.

They remained quiet after that, enjoying the peacefulness of the country. When they were nearly finished eating, Colin suddenly emerged from his carriage, looking more concerned than content. He headed toward them, a weary expression in his eyes. "Lily is not feeling well. The ride has been a bit much for her."

"I am sorry to hear that, darling. Is there anything we can do?" Elizabeth asked.

"Other than shorten the road so we can get there faster? I am afraid not. She will be fine once we reach Yorkshire. I just came to fetch her a few biscuits and some tea. She says she is not hungry, but I think some sustenance might help the queasiness."

"I will fix you a plate." Emily jumped up and piled several biscuits onto a china dish. She then fixed her brother a simple meal of one meat pie, four biscuits, and three hearty wedges of cheese. "Here," she said, handing the food to Colin. "This should satisfy you both."

"Thank you, Emily." He took the plates and turned to head back toward his carriage. He looked at Edmond. "Let us know the moment you are ready to depart."

"Yes, m'lord," Edmond said, as he checked on the horses.

After quickly eating her fill, Emily rose from the ground and made her way to the stream. She didn't dally like she normally did, mindful of Colin's report on Lily's state. After rinsing her hands in the water, she shook them, sending tiny water droplets flying all around her.

Then suddenly, she heard a twig snap.

She whirled around, her heart leaping to her throat. There was nothing behind her but the edge of a dense patch of bushes and trees. She let out a long, relieved breath. Perhaps some animal had scampered by, stepping on a fallen branch in its path. After waiting a few moments and hearing nothing more, she turned and faced the stream again.

"Emily!" The sound of her mother's voice pierced the stillness, causing her to startle once more.

"Coming!" Emily indelicately wiped the residual moisture from her hands on her skirt. Her mother would be appalled, but what she didn't know wouldn't hurt her. Emily took one more scrutinizing look at her surroundings, unable to shake the feeling that someone was watching . . . and she didn't think it was a simple woodland creature.

She shook her head, freeing herself of the paranoid thought. Who would be out here in the middle of nowhere? Especially spying on her? That didn't even approach sensibility. She knew better than to entertain such ridiculousness. As she made her way back to her family, she tried to think of a logical explanation as to why she was hearing things. Maybe the dreadful coach ride had jostled her brain one time too many.

"I have never been so glad to see Leton House," Elizabeth said wearily the next day as she looked out the window of the carriage. Emily followed suit, also grateful they had finally reached their destination. The trip had been more tiring than usual this year, despite the fact that they had stayed the previous night at a comfortable inn. Unfortunately they had arrived too late for Emily to ride Chandler. That would have to wait for the morning.

After unloading their baggage, fussing over Lily—who insisted she was fine and just needed to stretch her legs a bit—and partaking of a wonderful supper prepared by Estelle, whose talent greatly surpassed poor Isabel, their London chef, Emily went to the garden and sat on one of the stone benches. This was another special place for her. She had spent many a summer pruning her mother's rose bushes as her body drank in the warm sunshine. She examined the various flowers around her, breathing in their fragrant perfume. They were well kept, but could use a little extra tender loving care. She would do that tomorrow, after she had her morning ride. Right now she simply sat, enjoying the evening as dusk settled over the landscape before retreating inside for the night.

The next day she awoke early, donned her riding habit and headed for the stables, a scone in one hand and an apple in the other. She couldn't wait to see Chandler. He was now in the twilight of his years, but she considered him the gentlest of horses.

The thick aroma of hay and livestock reached her

nostrils when she entered the stables. She went to Chandler's stall and greeted him cheerfully. "Hello, lovey," she murmured, stroking his face. He nickered quietly, enjoying her attentions, as he always did. Her hand went to the pocket of her dress and she brought out a few sugar cubes and showed him the small apple. He gobbled them all up, then sniffed her pockets for more.

"Now, now, don't be a greedy sort." She laughed. "There is plenty more where that came from, but you will have to wait." She touched his velvety nose for a few moments. Then she looked around the stable, searching for Maynard, their part-time groom. Soon she found the redheaded young man and asked him to saddle her horse. When Chandler was ready, Maynard helped her into the saddle.

She tightened her grip on the reins and directed Chandler toward the nearby grove of trees. Above, light puffs of cottony clouds floated in the sky, with shafts of warm sunlight occasionally peeking out from behind them. The air temperature was perfect. A light breeze fluttered the leafy branches above her. She couldn't have asked for more ideal riding conditions.

She smiled, feeling happier than she had in a long time. She definitely needed this respite from London, she realized that now. Here her heart didn't ache as much over Gavin, her mind didn't ponder the possibilities with Charles, and Michael Balcarris didn't enter her thoughts. It was as if she hadn't a worry in the world, and it was a wonderful feeling.

Consumed with joy and freedom, she urged Chandler

to go faster as they exited the short patch of woods into a broad meadow. She gently slapped the reins against Chandler's neck, coercing him into a full gallop.

Suddenly she lurched forward. Everything inside her body rattled. Chandler had somehow lost his footing. Emily's body went numb as she realized her horse's legs were buckling under him. Automatically she yanked on the reins. But her grip wasn't tight enough. The leather straps slipped through her fingers. She hurtled from the horse just as he went down. She let out a loud scream. Her head hit the ground. Pain exploded behind her eyes.

Everything went black.

Chapter Ten

"I must say, that was quite an excruciating ride," Ruby sighed as Michael helped her out of the Hathery carriage. "I had forgotten how difficult journeying to the country could be."

Michael hadn't thought the trip to Leton House had been all that wearing. Granted he was used to travel and his mother was not. In his eagerness to reach Emily, he had also instructed their driver to hurry to Yorkshire, thus they had made the trip in record time. Looking at his fatigued mother, he realized he should have taken greater pains to ensure her comfort. However, he wasn't used to looking out for anyone but himself. That was painfully clear as he looked at his mother's exhausted face and watched her take a few steps on wobbly legs. Bless her heart though, she never uttered a word of complaint.

The front door to Leton House opened and out stepped Elizabeth. With quick steps she hurried toward them, surprise etched on her face.

"Ruby!" she exclaimed when she reached them. "You are the last person I expected to see!" She leaned forward and kissed her friend's cheek. "I am so delighted to have you here."

"Are you sure? I realize we have come unannounced—"

"Nonsense," Elizabeth said. "You are always welcome."

"Am I?" Michael said, stepping forward and lifting his quizzing glass. Uncertainty filtered through him, but he kept the emotion tightly shuttered.

Elizabeth deigned to give him a glance, but it was a curt one. Then she looked at Ruby, whose expression had suddenly tensed. Pressing her lips together for a brief moment, Elizabeth then turned to Michael. "For your mother's sake, you are welcome to stay here as long as she does. I would ask that you keep your distance from Emily, however. We are here to enjoy our holiday, not have it ruined."

Michael bowed deeply. "Thank you for your generosity. I will acquiesce to your request."

"Thank your mother. It is only on her behalf I offer it." She then ignored Michael as she put her arm around Ruby, focusing her attention on the weary woman. "You look positively exhausted, dear," Elizabeth said. "Come inside and I will fix you some tea. Have you eaten dinner yet?"

"Not yet. But I am feeling rather peckish. Perhaps I will have something light."

"Estelle has made some lovely pastries for breakfast. I know you will enjoy them." Elizabeth cast Michael one more caustic look, then guided Ruby to the house. "When we are finished eating, you can retire to the guest room and rest. Olive will have it ready for you. Michael can stay in the other spare room at the end of the hall."

As the women left, Michael peered at the house and grounds through his quizzing glass. Although it seemed he was alone, he never took that for granted, and studied everything within his purview. The place was familiar to him; he had stayed here a couple times in his youth when his family had visited the Dymoke's while on summer holiday. It was during those times that he and Colin, and later on Emily, had gotten into one form of mischief or another. He noticed it hadn't changed much in the past two decades. The house itself was small for a country estate, but had ample room for the family and a couple of guests. In the back of the house was the stable, where Colin's father had kept some prime horseflesh back in the day.

He remembered with fondness the times he and Colin had ridden out through the edge of a nearby forest, then a little bit further to a large meadow. He could still see young Emily following them on her horse, Chandler, trying the best she could to keep up with the boys. More often than not she had caught them, much to Colin's chagrin. Michael had never minded her tagging along, but Colin thought her a pest.

He also remembered the time he had rescued Emily and her cat. He had come upon Emily dangling from a high branch in the tree, perilously close to plunging to the ground. Stoic to the core, she didn't dissolve into hysterics or tears. She did yell for help upon seeing him. He hadn't hesitated to climb the tree and bring both her and her pet down. From that moment she had acted different toward him. Awkward, even. She hadn't yet blossomed into her own, and he had honestly looked upon her as a little sister at the time.

If only he could still see her that way. His life would be much simpler . . . and much less painful.

Yet, while his emotions had changed, Leton House had stayed the same, as if it has stood still in time. Back then, spending summers here as a young man, it would have never entered into Michael's mind that he would end up falling in love with Emily. Or that he would be a spy. He found himself longing for those simple days, when the biggest choice he had to make was whether he would take a ride before or after breakfast.

But he wasn't there to reminisce. He was there to talk to Colin about Pembrooke, and to warn Emily against the charlatan. He started toward the house, only to be knocked off balance when a young man ran past him, clipping him from behind.

"What ho there, lad?" he said, irritated by the boy's rudeness. "Have you forgotten your manners?"

The redheaded youth turned around, his pale expression filled with worry. "Beggin' your pardon, my lord," he said, jogging backwards. "But I must speak with Lord Chesreton immediately."

"Is there something wrong?" At the boy's wary expression, Michael added, "Do not worry, lad, you can tell me. I am a friend of the family."

He stopped in his tracks. "It is Miss Dymoke. Chandler has returned without her."

"What?" Michael cried.

"She left for her ride more than three hours ago. Never has she been gone that long. When the horse came back alone . . . I am worried something has happened to her."

Horror knotted inside him. "I hope to God you are wrong. Run, lad. Go tell Colin—Lord Chesreton—that Miss Dymoke is missing. Which direction did she go?"

"Toward the grove, my lord." Spinning around, he ran to the house.

Michael dashed to the stable and went to the first stall, which happened to house Triton, Colin's stallion. He snatched a saddle off its peg and within minutes had Triton ready to go. Leading the horse out, he hurled himself into the saddle and took off for the woods.

After making his way through the trees, he emerged into the meadow. He called out Emily's name as he slowed Triton to a walk, carefully making his way through the high, thick grass. If she had fallen off the horse in the meadow, he didn't want Triton to accidentally trample her. Inside his heart pounded against his chest until he thought it would burst. What if she were seriously injured? Or worse? He couldn't bear it if something happened to her. Desperately he redoubled his efforts and rapidly traversed the meadow.

Over and over he called her name. "Emily! Emily!"

He was near the end of the meadow when Triton stopped. Michael tried to urge him on, but he refused to budge. Trusting the horse's instincts, he jumped to the ground and started walking. Moments later he found her on the ground, her body completely still. "Dear God," he said, kneeling beside her.

She appeared to be dead.

"Emily. Emily . . ."

Emily kept hearing her name over and over. First it sounded far away, then nearer. Right now it seemed that whoever was saying it was practically on top of her. She fought to open her eyes, but it was difficult. Her head was pounding, and her body ached all over. Vaguely she remembered Chandler tripping and her falling off his back, but the details were hazy. It was as if she were in a dream world of some sort.

"Please . . . wake up, sweetheart."

Sweetheart? Now she knew she had to be dreaming. No one she could think of would call her sweetheart. Except for her mother, but Elizabeth actually preferred the term *darling* as an endearment. Emily had never heard anyone use the word *sweetheart* in her presence, especially a male.

Then she felt someone's hands on her body, touching her shoulders, then her arms, then moving down to her legs . . .

Her eyes flew open. Fear struck every chord inside her. Instinctively she lifted up her arms, curled her hands into fists, and started flailing away. "Let me go!" She screamed as loud as she could, hoping someone, anyone would hear her and come to her rescue. "Leave me alone!"

"Wait, Emily. Hold on just a moment—"

The voice sounded familiar, but she didn't care. Someone was taking advantage of her. She wasn't about to let him have his way without a fight.

"Emily, stop! Stop right now!"

Strong hands gripped her wrists, forcing her still. The grip was firm, but didn't cause her pain. As a result of her fall and thrashing around, her hat had become dislodged, along with her hair. Peering through a curtain of blond wisps, she looked at the man in front of her. When she realized who he was, her mouth dropped open in shock.

"Emily?" Michael asked. His was speech was slow and deliberate, as he thought she'd never heard her name before. "Are you all right?"

His question was possibly the most stupid one ever posed in the history of history. Of course she wasn't all right. She hurt. All over. She'd been thrown from her horse, scared out of her wits, and now found herself in shambles with Michael Balcarris clutching her wrists. She planned to tell him exactly these thoughts and more, but all she could manage was a weak, "Yes."

"Thank God. Now, listen to me carefully. I am going to let you go. Please, if you can, refrain from pummeling me further. I cannot help you if you insist on physically abusing me."

She almost laughed at his comment. Perhaps she'd hit her head harder than she thought, because he seemed different to her. No haughtiness. No silly accent. No expression of boredom. Instead he seemed . . . concerned. Very concerned, actually.

He let go of her hands and sat back on his heels. "I already know you can move your arms. How about your legs? Do you think anything is broken?"

She wiggled her toes in her slippers, gradually bent one knee, then the other. "No. I do not think so."

"Very good. Now, I am going to help you stand. If you feel dizzy, tell me." He placed one hand underneath her arm, then another at her waist. "On the count of three. Ready?"

She nodded and he hoisted her up. Not an easy feat, considering she wasn't exactly a lightweight. Once she was upright, however, she stopped thinking about the pudginess of her body as the world started spinning. There was nothing she could do but lean against him for support.

"Lightheaded?"

"Quite," she said before closing her eyes. But that didn't help. If anything, it made things worse. She still felt as if someone were twirling her nonstop.

"Do you want to sit down again?"

The pain in her head intensified, and it seemed her head would split in two right there in the meadow. Tears, unbidden and unwanted, especially in Michael's presence, slid down her face. "No. I do not want to sit down. I just want to go home."

Without another word, he lifted her in his arms and carried her to his horse. Again, he did this with little effort, and he carried her as if she weighed next to nothing. She had no idea he was so strong. She could feel the hardness of his upper arm against her lower back. She also had no idea he smelled so good. Why hadn't she noticed that before, considering how many times they had danced together? Granted, she had tried her very best not to give him anything more than her unqualified divided attention, which was perhaps the reason why she had never realized that he smelled absolutely amazing. She leaned her head against his shoulder, inhaling his scent. It was indisputably male, not the cloying cologne most of the dandies wore. A tiny flutter whirred in her belly, a sensation she felt clear down to her toenails.

Now she knew her brain had been damaged in the fall. She was sniffing Michael, for goodness' sake!

Opening her eyes and trying get her mind off of the outlandish thoughts running through her head, she focused on the horse Michael had ridden. She could see he had used Colin's horse, Triton. Suddenly a rational thought pierced through the insanity. Michael was in Yorkshire. At her family's summer home, a place he hadn't visited for years. "What are you doing here?" she asked, bewildered. "Aren't you supposed to be in London?"

"Do not worry about that at the moment," Michael

said. "Tell me, how are you feeling right now? That is what's important."

She felt dizzy. Most definitely dizzy. But she wasn't sure if it was because of the blow to her head or the fact that in spite of everything, including common sense, she was quite enjoying having Michael's muscular arms around her. "I am not quite myself," she managed. It was possibly the most understated comment she'd ever made in her life.

"That is to be expected. From what I can tell, you took quite a serious fall. We will be home soon enough."

She closed her eyes again. Home sounded wonderful. Suddenly all she wanted to do was lie down in her own bed and wish the pain away.

He set her gently in the saddle, keeping his hand on her waist. Then he hauled himself up behind her. "Lean back," he said. When she hesitated, he added, "Do not worry. I will not let you fall."

Clearly, she was all mixed up. Emily was certain that in a few moments she would wake up from the dream she was having. Because this had to be a dream. It simply wasn't possible that the tender, kind man who was holding her against his chest as he expertly rode back to Leton House was Michael Balcarris. He merely happened to look like him. And wear the same absurd clothing. And know exactly how to get back to her house.

Shutting her eyes again, she became too tired to question the situation any more. His arm curled about her waist and he held her firm. For that she was thankful.

She'd already had one spill off a horse today. She certainly didn't need another one.

She didn't know how long they had ridden, but they finally reached Leton House. With great effort she lifted one eyelid up. She could see Colin standing there, reaching up for her. He grasped her and helped her down to the ground, then put his arm around her shoulders. She slumped against him, grateful to be home.

As he led her up the stairs, she heard him call out over his shoulder, "Thank you, Michael."

She stiffened. Michael? He had rescued her after all.

Chapter Eleven

"Y ou are looking much better, darling," Elizabeth said as she handed Emily a steaming cup of tea. "I believe in a few days you will be right as rain."

"I am right as rain," Emily retorted. She was also going stir-crazy. Three days of confinement for a mere bump on the head had become torturous. She was supposed to be enjoying her holiday, not spending it cooped up inside her room. While she had been thankful at the time of her fall for the safety and comfort of her bed, now that she was healing, it felt as if she were serving a prison sentence. She was sitting next to the window, which only intensified her torture. Everything she wanted was out of reach.

Elizabeth raised a scolding brow as she sipped her tea. "You must be feeling better as well," she said drolly. "Your sweet disposition has returned."

"Sorry." Emily blew across the teacup, sending rippling waves over the beverage. "It is just that I feel fine, Mama. The bump has receded and my headache has disappeared. I do not understand why I still cannot go outside."

"Because you took a terrible fall, Emily. People have died from less, as Dr. Colgan so bluntly explained after he examined you. I simply want to make sure you are completely well before you go gallivanting about again."

"I know, Mama, I know. And I do appreciate your concern." Emily leaned back against the chaise and looked out the window with longing. The sun shone with full strength, and the gently sloping hills surrounding Leton House seemed to call out her name. She wasn't about to let a fall prevent her from enjoying the country she loved so much. "I fear I may go crazy if I do not get out soon," she murmured.

"What was that, darling?"

She turned to her mother. "If I promise to behave and stay in my room for the rest of the day, then may I go outside tomorrow?" She sounded like a small child negotiating for a later bedtime, but desperate times called for desperate measures.

Elizabeth paused, took another sip of tea, set the delicate cup on the small table in front of the chaise, and turned to her daughter. "I suppose. However, you must promise not to ride your horse."

"But Mama—"

"At least not for another week." She held up her hand as Emily started to protest again. "You may be an adult, my daughter, but I am still your mother, and I have your best interests at heart. What if you have a dizzy spell and take another tumble?"

"I doubt that would happen."

"I do too, if you wait a week. Now, do not even contemplate a way to change my mind, because I will not. My decision is final."

"All right." It wasn't what Emily had in mind, but at least it was something.

"I believe I have some news that might cheer you up," Elizabeth said. "There is someone who wants to see you."

"Really?" Emily wracked her brain trying to figure out who her mother was referring to. Then she remembered she was expecting a visitor. "Is it Charles?"

"No. Mr. Pembrooke isn't here. Did he say when he would arrive?"

"Not specifically. He merely said he would be coming soon."

"Then I am sure he will be here. He strikes me as a man who keeps his word. And while I am sure when he does arrive he will be very happy to see you, I am not referring to him."

"Then who? Lily? Colin?" While she wouldn't mind their company, she didn't particularly think their desire to see her would cause her mother to play guessing games.

"No, no. It is Michael, darling. He's been most anxious to check on your welfare."

She looked out the window again, a familiar feeling

of bewilderment churning inside her. It was still difficult to wrap her mind around the fact that Michael was
her rescuer. The entire scene played out as a blur in her
mind, as if it had all been a dream and she had been an
observer, not a participant. The man had looked like
Michael Balcarris, but certainly hadn't acted like him.
He had been kind, attentive, strong—everything Michael
was not. It was most puzzling indeed.

"Emily, I know I have not been very cordial to
Michael for quite a long time. To be honest, if he had
disappeared off the face of the earth a few days ago I
would not have been too upset."

Emily whipped around and stared at her mother.
Elizabeth had never been one to utter such a harsh
statement. "Mama, I am shocked you would say such a
thing."

"I know, but I cannot help the way I felt."

"You never told me what he did to make you so angry."

Elizabeth ran her finger around her teacup for a few
moments, then turned to Emily. She let out a sigh. "Remember when I went over to Ruby's to speak to her
about a match between you and Michael?"

"Yes," Emily said emphatically. Her mother had returned in a heated rage, claiming that there would never
be a match between Emily and Michael. Emily had
thought herself the receiver of a special gift that day
when her mother put an end to that preposterous notion.

"What I did not tell you was that Michael had been
most insulting. Toward you."

A sharp pang pierced Emily's heart. She had never

held back from hurling insults and harsh words at Michael. And it didn't dawn on her until now that he had never reciprocated, even when she deserved it. He could be exasperating, and occasionally he would make a sharp quip, but not one that ever caused her anything more than irritation. She had assumed he had been as unfeeling on the inside as he appeared on the outside. Her reaction to finding out that he did speak ill of her, and in the presence of her mother, no less, stunned her. She shouldn't care what he thought of her.

But for some reason, she did.

"What did he say?" she asked, gripping the side of her chair.

"It does not matter what he said, not any more," Elizabeth replied. She walked behind Emily and put her hands on her daughter's shoulders. "I realize now the things he said that day were lies. What I mean is I knew they were lies at the time, but now I believe he believes they are lies too."

Emily frowned. She couldn't make heads or tails out of her mother's words. "Please, Mama. You are making me dizzy."

"Sorry, love. At any rate, do not concern yourself with what he said. What matters is what he did for you. He brought you back to us."

"Mama, I fell off a horse. I did not disappear into some unfathomable mist."

Elizabeth rubbed Emily's shoulders. "I realize that, but if he had not found you . . . I dread to think of what might have happened. You could have been attacked by wolves, for goodness' sake. I cannot think of a worse fate."

If there was one animal Elizabeth Dymoke was afraid of, it was a wolf. Her fear ran so deep she couldn't abide dogs, not even the little lap dogs favored by several of the ladies of the *ton*. "I seriously doubt I would have been at the mercy of a wolf pack."

"Nevertheless, something horrible could have happened to you, and Michael prevented it. Not only that, he has expressed much concern for you. Almost hourly, I must say. After Dr. Colgan arrived, I believe he paced the floor as much as Colin did."

Emily found that difficult to believe, but she didn't contradict her mother. "So you have forgiven him, then, for impugning me?"

"Absolutely." She rose from her seat and moved toward the doorway. "He really is a hero, you know."

Emily rolled her eyes. And her brother thought she was the dramatic one in the family.

"I will let Michael know you are ready to see him."

"Now?"

"Emily, don't be ridiculous. Or so stubborn. He at least deserves your gratitude."

Well, she couldn't very well argue with that. He did help her, that was for sure. And her mother was right, she could at least thank him for that. "All right. I will be down to see him."

"Splendid. I will let him know."

Once her mother had left, Emily stood up and went to her vanity. She looked at herself in the mirror. She frowned at her image, as she usually did when she spied her rounded cheeks and face. But this time she scrutinized her reflection. The bruise from the bump on her head was still visible on the corner of her forehead, but other than that, she seemed to have suffered no ill effects from her fall, save for sore shoulders. It was really fortunate that she hadn't been more seriously hurt.

She thought back to that day, as she had so often since the accident. There were so many things she didn't understand, especially about Michael. He had been almost unrecognizable, but yet very familiar. She recalled when she had first regained consciousness after knocking her head on the ground. She had thought she was being molested, when in actuality he had been checking for broken bones.

Then she suddenly remembered something she had forgotten up to that moment.

He had called her sweetheart. An incomprehensible shiver of warmth coursed through at the memory.

Yes, there was the possibility she could have imagined it. But through the haze of her reminiscence, that one single word came shining through bright and clear.

Michael Balcarris had called her sweetheart.

Michael sat in the small but tastefully decorated drawing room in Leton House. He lounged casually on one of the high-backed chairs, his legs crossed at the knees, one arm draping the back of the chair, as if he didn't have a care in the world as he waited for Emily to come downstairs.

Inside, however, was a different story. He had spent the past three days worrying over Emily while trying not to show too much interest in her condition. By the second day, however, he realized he hadn't fooled Elizabeth at all. Since Emily's fall, her mother had treated him differently, as if she had never been angry with him at all. She had also thanked him profusely for taking care of her daughter. Knowing that his relationship with Elizabeth had been repaired did help ease his mind somewhat. He just wished it hadn't had come at such a cost to Emily.

The second day after Emily's accident, his worry for her had abated. Fortunately she seemed to be healing quickly from her fall, and didn't seem to suffer any other ill effects. It was a miracle, truly. He had never felt such panic in his life as when he'd seen her lying prone on the ground, motionless. For an instant he had actually thought she was dead. He had been thankful beyond belief when he discovered she wasn't.

But he had gained a new worry. Upon further reflection of the events, he realized that he had forgotten himself when he found Emily. Panic and dread had caused him to forget about his foppery. When she had awakened, all he thought about was making sure she was okay and getting her medical attention.

What if she noticed? How would he explain it to her if she started asking questions? He hoped against hope that she wouldn't remember, and if she did, not remember clearly. He would be in a fine mess indeed if she did.

"Hello, Michael."

At the sound of her voice, he turned and looked at the doorway. She strolled in, a vision of beauty. Her hair was fashioned in a simple knot at the nape of her neck, and the candy pink color of her dress highlighted her fair coloring. The ample sway of her hips as she moved nearly drove him crazy. Quickly he grasped his quizzing glass and held it in front of him like a shield as he rose from his chair. "Good morning, Miss Dymoke. I am most gratified to see you up and about."

"Thank you, Michael." She entered the room and walked toward him. He could see the light bruising on her forehead where she sustained her injury. "I also want to thank you for your timely appearance after my fall. I do not know what I would have done if you hadn't shown up."

"It was nothing. I assure you."

"No, no, it was definitely something, and I appreciate you being there for me."

Michael relaxed a little bit. Things appeared to be back to normal between them. Well, perhaps a little abnormal, considering her polite attitude toward him. He had no doubts that in a few moments he would say something to annoy her and she would tell him off. That was a verbal dance he was used to. Not this benign, almost friendly, conversation.

"I am glad you are feeling well, Miss Dymoke. Now, if you will excuse me, I must take my leave. I promised Mother I would walk with her in the rose garden."

"I just saw Lady Hathery and Mama having tea in the

dining room," Emily said, moving closer to him. "So it seems you have a bit of time before your outing. I would like to ask you some questions, if you do not mind."

"If you must." Alarm flashed within him. Now she was being too polite. But to refuse her would raise her suspicions even further. With a sigh, he sat down on the chair and tapped his quizzing glass against his hand. Maybe if he irritated her enough she would give up and leave off her inquisition.

"I have been wondering about a few things since the accident," she said, sitting down in a chair directly across from him.

He brought his quizzing glass to his eye. "You have?" His tone dripped with contrived insincerity. "I cannot fathom the ideas that flow through your little mind."

Her expression lost some of it complacency with that remark. He was loath to hurt her, but better for her to be off balance than him.

"My little mind, as you call it, remembered something you said. When I woke up after my fall."

"Your name? I do recall saying that a few times. Other than that . . ." he let his voice trail into silence.

She shook her head. "Not just my name. One other word." She looked him directly in the eye. "One . . . interesting . . . word."

The look in her eyes nearly undid him. Confidence, as if she held something over him. Frantically he tried to remember all he had said to her that day, but couldn't recall anything out of the ordinary. Mostly he had repeated her name. Clearly, however, he had said something else. And because he couldn't remember what it was, a knot of acute anxiety formed in his belly. He clutched his quizzing glass and forced a haughty lift of his brow as he tamped down the disturbing emotion. Maybe if he knew what he'd said he could come up with a plausible excuse for saying it. Or a decent denial. Either one would work for him at this point. "Now, now, Miss Dymoke," said, thankful his voice didn't belie his internal struggle. "Do not keep me in suspense much longer. I do not have time for these silly games. What exactly did I say?"

"Sweetheart," she replied, a sly smile spreading across her lovely face. "You, Michael Balcarris, called me sweetheart."

Chapter Twelve

"I most certainly did not call you sweetheart."

Emily hid a chuckle at Michael's vehement protest. She had hit the mark, judging from the reddish hue appearing on his cheeks and his sudden shifting in his seat. "You most certainly did. I remember it clearly."

"Miss Dymoke, the only thing clear to me is that you are suffering from a delusion. Not to be, ah, unexpected, considering the size of the bump on your head."

"Oh, Michael, why be so formal? If you can call me sweetheart, surely you can call me Emily."

"Miss Dymoke," he said, with emphasis, "for the last time, I did not call you sweetheart. I would never use such a word . . . especially with you."

Ordinarily Emily would have taken umbrage to such a cutting remark, but this time there was a difference. She suddenly realized it was much more fun to tease

Michael than to fight with him. When she argued with him, he always seemed to have the upper hand, never failing to remain calm while her blood nearly reached the boiling point. But for all his protestations and his attempts at being nonchalant and unaffected, she could tell by the white-knuckled grip he had on his quizzing glass that he was uncomfortable. Very uncomfortable. It was an interesting predicament to witness.

"Oh, come now, Michael. No need to be bashful." She rose and walked toward him, stopping a few steps in front of him.

He leaned back in his chair, giving her a dubious look. "You are talking in riddles, Emily. Perhaps you hit your head harder than was first realized."

"No, no, Michael. I know exactly what I am saying. And to think, all this time I never knew."

"Never knew what?" He held the quizzing glass between them, as if he was tempted to swat her with it.

Oh, she was enjoying this. A pin prick of guilt jabbed at her, but she shoved it away. She knew she shouldn't be taunting him like this, but she couldn't help herself. It had been so long since she'd seen any emotion out of him at all. Seeing him squirm as she moved closer to him was too much to resist. "All this time I never knew you cared."

"Of course I care. You are my mother's best friend's daughter."

"That is not what I mean—"

"If it had been anyone else lying unconscious in the meadow I would have done the same thing." His features hardened. "Do not think yourself so special, Miss Dymoke. Because I certainly do not."

Pain sliced within her heart. This time his harsh words did hit home. Teasing him had been a mistake. Obviously she couldn't match wits with him. She never had been able to.

She hated being at his mercy like this, never knowing whether his next remark would cut her to the quick. Normally she would fight back, escalate the argument into a full-blown shouting match, naturally with her doing all of the shouting.

Her shoulders slumped. For once, she didn't have the desire to fight back anymore. She was tired of being at odds with him. Obviously nothing she said to him would change anything. He would continue to be the same self-absorbed knave he'd always been. She couldn't make him revert back to the fun-loving Michael she'd known in the past. Perhaps he was correct after all, and she had truly imagined he called her sweetheart. As he said himself, she wasn't anything special. She'd known that all along.

Why she wasted her time talking to him at all was beyond her comprehension.

Straightening her shoulders, she looked at him. For some peculiar reason she couldn't pull her gaze away. Maybe it had to do with the injury she had recently sustained, but his callous attitude had affected her deeply this time, much more than normal. Blast, now she was on the verge of tears.

Not that she would ever cry in front of him. She

didn't need to provide him with anymore hurtful ammunition. He could wound her very nicely on his own. Swallowing the lump in her throat, she fortified her resolve. "Mama pointed out that I should be grateful to you for bringing me back to Leton House, and that I should express that gratitude in person. So consider yourself thanked. Now, if you will excuse me."

Spinning on her heel, she turned to leave the room. As she reached the threshold, Michael's voice halted her steps.

"Emily . . . wait."

He'd said her name. Not Miss Dymoke, but Emily. Other than the day of the accident, he hadn't called her by her first name since they were young. That alone gave her pause.

Despite that, however, she should have ignored him. But there was something in his voice that compelled her to find out what he wanted. Slowly she turned around, her posture ramrod straight, her chin lifted in defiance. Fortunately it hadn't taken long to collect herself. She didn't want to show weakness of any kind.

He lowered his quizzing glass and stood, looking a bit sheepish. "Perhaps I was, um, a tad bit too harsh."

Emily crossed her arms over her chest. "A tad?"

Michael cleared his throat. "Yes. A tad. Everyone is special . . . in their own way, of course. It was bad form of me to say otherwise."

She digested his words. Apologizing wasn't exactly in his repertoire, but at least he'd had a decent go at it. She had to give him credit for trying. Oddly enough, his simple admission had eased her resentment almost entirely. "Michael Balcarris, are you actually saying you're sorry?"

"Ah," Michael said, lifting the glass to his face. "You may call it that, if you wish."

"Where is pen and paper? I must mark this momentous occasion for posterity. The day Michael actually admitted he was wrong. I never thought I would live to see it happen."

"Now you are being silly."

"Why, yes. Yes, I am." She strode toward him, experiencing a freedom in his presence she hadn't felt before. He had actually apologized to her. Which meant there was hope for him yet. "Tell me, Michael. Haven't you ever had the urge to be silly?"

"Hardly," Michael said with a sniff. "I have no desire to behave immaturely."

"But why not? What is wrong with having a little fun?" She smiled. "Or even a lot of fun?"

He averted his gaze. "Do not be ridiculous. We are adults, not children."

She ignored his statement of the obvious. "I think I know what your problem is, Michael. You have forgotten how to have fun."

"I have not. I have plenty of joviality in my life."

"Oh, really? I am afraid I do not quite believe you. Why don't you tell me what you do for fun then."

"I, ah, well, I—"

"See, you cannot even come up with one thing. You have spent so many years being pretentious and off-putting that you've completely overlooked the lighter side of life." Without thinking too much about it, she went to him and put her hand on his arm. "But I know how we can fix that. I know exactly how we can put some *joie de vivre* back into your dreary life."

He eyed her suspiciously.

"You, Lord Hathery, are taking me on a picnic."

"Bah!" he scoffed, walking past her. "You must be joking. You and I? Having a picnic? Together?"

"No, I am not joking. And yes, we are going on a picnic." The more she thought about it, the more she warmed up to the idea. She was tired of being stuck in the house, and Michael definitely needed a little levity in his stuffy life. A picnic would be a perfect solution to both. Perhaps the activity would make him slightly tolerable. "We will have a lovely feast, with plenty of delicious treats. Then after we eat, you and I will play a game."

He turned and faced her, peering down the length of his nose. "I do not play games, Miss Dymoke."

"You used to."

Her words seemed to give him pause. "That was a long time ago."

"Too long, I am afraid. Come now, Michael, it is not as if I am asking you to poke yourself with stick pins or go swimming naked in the Thames on a winter's day. All I want is for you to join me for an afternoon picnic and a game or two. I promise you will have a splendid time."

"I seriously doubt it." He looked at her once more, then sighed as if he had given up. "Very well. I shall accompany you. There is something I wanted to discuss with you anyway. I suppose I can do so while we are lunching."

"That is the spirit. I will have Estelle prepare a basket, and I will meet you at the stables in an hour."

"One moment," he said, holding up his limp-wristed hand. "I do not think your mother would approve of you going out today. Especially on a horse."

"Fine. We will walk then. And let me take care of Mama. I do not think she will mind me taking some recreation in the least, especially since I will be with you. You have proved yourself most trustworthy in her eyes, Michael." She glided past him and flashed a smile. "I will see you in exactly one hour, Lord Hathery. Don't be late!"

Exactly one hour later, Michael appeared at the stables. He'd hoped Emily had come to her senses and decided against having a picnic, or at the very least her mother had said no to the idea. Unfortunately, he saw her standing there with Olive, one of the Dymoke's servants, who apparently had been designated as their chaperone. From the scowl on her face, he assumed she wasn't too happy about the designation. Emily, seemingly unaware of her gloomy companion, had a picnic basket in her hand and a smile on her face.

Michael suppressed a long-suffering sigh. There was nothing he could do about this except to make the best of the situation. If he tried to back out again she would pester him until he acquiesced. At least he could turn this to his advantage; he could speak to her about Pembrooke in relative privacy.

But if his surface behavior displayed discomfiture at the idea of spending time with Emily, his inner being believed otherwise. He had agreed to her request not because he wanted to discuss Pembrooke or because Emily had a particular penchant for beleaguering her target until she got her way. He felt he had no other choice but to go with her. Perhaps it was the glint of mischief he'd seen in her eyes when she was teasing him, a glint he had caused to fade when he had told her she wasn't anything special. That time he had gone too far with the remark. Her pain had become his pain, and he had to apologize. From there the conversation had gotten away from him, and now he found himself facing an afternoon in her company.

If normal circumstances were to prevail, he would have been more than happy to picnic with her. The fact that she wanted to be in his presence was enough to celebrate, and deep in his heart he could think of nothing sweeter than to spend time with Emily.

However, he couldn't remember the last time circumstances resembled anything close to normalcy.

Chapter Thirteen

"Smashing picnic."

Emily heard Olive's mumbled, sarcastic words, and she might have been offended by the servant's assessment of the afternoon if it hadn't been so accurate. Even more exasperating was that only fifteen minutes had passed since she, Michael, and Olive had arrived at their picnic spot.

They were picnicking in a small clearing behind Leton House. The afternoon couldn't have been lovelier, weather-wise. The sky was clear and blue, the sun was bright and warm, and the grass was fragrant and soft. Emily had had such high hopes for the outing, but she should have known better where Michael was concerned. So far it had been the most boring afternoon of her life. It seemed that Michael was singularly determined to be even duller than usual.

Olive rose from the edge of the picnic blanket and walked over to one of the slender trees at the edge of the stream. She leaned against the back of the trunk and closed her eyes, stretching her long, thin legs in front of her. Her dusty brown shoes peeked out from underneath a gray work dress. Emily knew her mother would have had a fit if she had witnessed Olive shirking her chaperone duties in favor of a nap, but Emily couldn't blame her. It wasn't as if the young woman had anything to worry about. Michael was about as dangerous as a rag doll.

He hadn't uttered more than two words since they left the house, despite his earlier declaration that he had wanted to talk to her. Because he was a gentleman, he had dutifully carried the basket, picked their spot, spread out the blanket, and served lunch. With awkward movements he had lowered himself to the blanket and remained there, sitting stiffly, his overblown cravat fluttering slightly in the breeze. He had nibbled on a few of Estelle's delectable treats, then spent the rest of the time gazing at his fingernails.

This was not fun. Not fun at all.

Finally, after several uncomfortable moments, he spoke. "There is something I must tell you, Miss Dymoke."

Back to her formal name again. She should have known not to expect anything different. "What is it?" she asked half-heartedly.

"It concerns Mr. Pembrooke. He is not who he seems to be."

"Really." She didn't bother to stifle a yawn.

"I have good reason to believe he is only interested in you for your money."

Emily shrugged off his words. She refused to be baited into another argument. He'd insulted her again, insinuating that no man would be interested in her for her, but because of her dowry. However, she wasn't going to fight back. "If that is all he wants, then fine by me."

"What?" he sounded genuinely surprised. "You would marry a man who does not love you?"

"As you said yourself, I am nothing special." Despite her attempts at acting blasé, she did feel a small measure of hurt inside that Charles had ulterior motives for paying attention to her. Yet a part of her didn't think she could take Michael seriously. He might have only said that about Charles to get a rise out of her. She wouldn't give him the satisfaction. She rose from the blanket. "I suppose you think I should be grateful someone is interested in me at all."

"That is not what I meant."

"It doesn't matter, Michael." She looked down at him. "I do not want to talk about Charles. Let us play a game instead," she said, desperate to change the subject. The last thing she wanted to do was discuss her shortcomings with Michael.

"I would rather not. As I stated before, I do not play games."

Emily crouched down in front of him. "You used to. I recall how you and Colin and I used to hide from each other. Then we would search all over, trying to track each other down. And if I remember correctly, I ran faster than both of you."

Shrugging, he said. "Child's play. That's all it was." He started picking at his fingernails again.

This wasn't working out at all. Emily sighed. Drastic times called for drastic measures, and she was about to do something drastic indeed. Glancing at Olive, she saw that the woman was dead asleep. Quickly, before she lost her nerve, she batted off Michael's hat, took his quizzing glass and tossed it in a nearby bush, then grabbed his cravat and started untying it.

"Em—wha—now look here—"

It took a little bit of doing, but she had the element of surprise on her side. By the time Michael had reached up to grab her hands she had loosened the cravat enough to pull it off of him. She sprung up from the blanket and started running, waving the long white strip of cloth in the air.

"If you want it back, you will have to catch me!"

"Now see here," Michael called out, rising most inelegantly and almost toppling over. Before he had gotten his footing, she picked up her skirts with her free hand and took off running alongside the creek.

At some point, her hat fell off, and she felt several pins slide out of her hair. Still holding the cravat high above her head, she let it trail behind her like a kite's tail. For a few moments she thought her movements were in vain, that he had given up the chase, too dignified and boring to indulge in anything more taxing than sleeking back his hair. But soon she heard the pounding of Michael's footsteps behind her. Clutching her skirts tighter, she quickened her speed.

She had just passed a curve in the stream when she felt his fingertips brush her back. With a squeal she jerked away from him, cutting to the left. That ended up being a mistake, as he suddenly grabbed her around the waist, pulled her back against his chest, and flung her around in a semi-circle.

Her breath left her body in an exhilarating puff of air. For the briefest of seconds, it felt like she was floating as she spun in his arms and faced him. Then somehow he lost his footing and fell, dragging her on top of him.

They ended up practically nose to nose. She gasped for air. It had been a considerable amount of time since she'd run so hard, and she had been a much smaller girl at the time. Her chest heaving, she gazed at his face.

A shiver slid through her body. She'd never been this close to him before. Yes, they'd danced together numerous times over the years, but he had always held her at arm's length, and she had been so consistently irritated with him that she'd paid scant attention to his physicality before this. But now, with them both breathing so hard they could barely move, she took the time to really look at him.

She realized, with such a short distance between them, that there was nothing foppish about him. Perhaps it was the fact that he was concentrating on catching his breath, but his cheeks no longer looked sunken, his lips no longer pursed. His green eyes were filled with mirth, something she hadn't seen in him for ages. His normally perfectly coiffed brown hair poked up in places from the exertion and fall, and a heavy lock of it had fallen over his forehead. She had the irresistible urge to brush it away. "Now," she said with a smile, still breathless. "Wasn't that fun?"

She felt his arm tighten around her waist, and her smile faded. So did the mirth from his eyes. It was replaced by a darkening intensity, one that she felt clear to the tips of her toes. A fluttering erupted in her stomach as he continued to look at her. Then his gaze dropped to her mouth. Her heart performed a tiny flip in her chest. Why was he looking at her that way? It almost seemed as if he wanted to kiss her. Her heartbeat intensified. The very thought of his lips touching hers sent an inexplicable wave of excitement surging throughout her entire being.

Then he abruptly shoved her to the side, off his body. She landed on the ground in an inelegant heap. Sitting up, he grabbed his cravat, snatching it from her grasp. "That was certainly *not* fun," he snapped, wrapping the cloth around his neck. He stood and brushed the grass off his expensive breeches with sharp swipes of his hands. Straightening his coat, he looked down at her. "Our picnic, Miss Dymoke, is over." With that he turned around and stormed off, heading in the direction of Leton House.

Emily sat up and shoved a couple of errant strands of hair from her face, more confused than ever. For a few minutes she was certain he'd enjoyed their chase. She thought he enjoyed her capture even more. She certainly did, something she'd never dreamed even possible. Her heart was still pounding, and she knew it wasn't from the running. The look he had given her when they were on the ground had made her toes curl.

But this was Michael! How could she be having such thoughts about him? True, she had wanted him to lighten up a little bit. And she might have gone a little too far in her pursuit of such amusement when she relieved him of his cravat. But her intentions had never gone any further than having a bit of merriment. Then suddenly she was thinking about kissing him! How positively ridiculous—not to mention it was beyond the realm of plausibility. She reached up and touched the still tender spot on her head. That had to be the reason why the act of kissing and Michael Balcarris would be in her thoughts at the same time.

Still, for all her protestations, she couldn't put the idea out of her mind. And she couldn't quiet the fluttering in her belly every time she thought about her lips touching his. Despite knowing that it wouldn't and shouldn't happen, she continued to imagine what it would be like to kiss him. That brought even more exciting emotions to the surface. Emotions she'd never felt with Gavin, and certainly never with Charles. Emotions she didn't want to stop experiencing.

"Miss Dymoke!"

Olive's panicked voice carried from the distance, jerking Emily out of her musings. Emily stood, brushed off her dress, and tried to smooth her hair. On the way back to the picnic site, she found her hat, and pinned it back on her head with slightly shaking hands. Hopefully she didn't look too disheveled. The last thing she wanted to do was raise Olive's suspicions.

When Olive saw her, she appeared on the verge of tears. "A thousand pardons, miss, I am so sorry. I only meant to close my eyes for a few moments. Please forgive me for my neglect."

"That is quite all right," Emily said reassuringly. Even if Olive had noticed anything different about Emily, she doubted the woman would have said as much. As it was, Olive looked completely consumed with her own distress. Emily was thankful for small favors, as she herself was confused enough over the afternoon's events. She didn't want to have to explain anything to Olive as well.

"Again, I am truly sorry." Olive's gaze darted back and forth as she searched the picnic area. "Where is Lord Hathery?"

"He had to return to the house."

"Thank goodness," she said, sounding most relieved. "I mean, sorry about that, Miss Dymoke. I know you were looking forward to a nice afternoon." Olive turned around and began packing up the leftovers from the picnic. The food had hardly been touched. "I hope you both had a lovely time." She might have meant to be sincere, but her tone was filled with doubt.

Emily bent down to help her clean up. Although their

picnic hadn't turned out exactly as she had expected, she wasn't altogether disappointed. "Let us just say we had an interesting time." She glanced in the direction Michael had taken off. "An interesting time, indeed."

Chapter Fourteen

Emily paced the length of her bedroom, unable to get Michael out of her mind.

She supposed she shouldn't be surprised at her exasperation with him, since he had exasperated her on a continual basis for several years. But she was more than disturbed by the cause of her consternation. Their picnic had concluded hours ago, but she still couldn't shake the image of his face as he had gazed at her mouth after he had captured her. She also couldn't release the thought of how much she had wanted him to kiss her.

Striding to her bedroom window, she looked outside, watching the last rays of the golden sun dip below the horizon. She couldn't spend the rest of the night like this. She had to talk to someone. Only one person came to mind—Lily.

Emily left the bedroom in search of her sister-in-law. Lily had taken to spending evenings in her and Colin's suite of rooms, so she started there. She knocked quietly on the door. "Lily? Are you there?"

"Yes, Emily. Do come in."

Lily's voice sounded weaker than normal, but Emily chalked it up to an expectant mother's weariness at the end of the day. She opened the door and saw Lily seated on a small sofa, her long legs stretched out in front of her, her eyes closed. Emily suddenly felt guilty for disturbing her.

"I can come back another time, if you prefer," Emily said.

Lily opened her eyes. "No, no, that's quite all right. I would like the company, actually. Colin is downstairs playing cards with Elizabeth and Ruby, although I imagine he'll want a reprieve in a short while."

Emily nodded, visualizing her brother's valiant attempts at feigning interest in spending an evening entertaining his mother and her best friend.

With great effort, Lily sat up straighter on the sofa. She tilted her head as she looked at Emily. "Is everything all right? You look preoccupied."

"I am." Emily sat in a comfortable high-backed chair across from Lily. "I don't even know where to begin."

Lily smiled slightly. "How about at the beginning?"

Thinking that was as good advice as any, Emily told Lily everything, starting with the fall from her horse and Michael's rescue up until the end of their picnic, including their almost-kiss.

After hearing Emily's tale, Lily's lips pursed into an O-shape. "Goodness," she finally said.

"Goodness? Is that all you have to say?"

"Emily, you must give me a moment to take all of this in."

Leaning back in the chair, Emily blew out a puff of air. "Of course. Sorry for sounding snippy. It is just that I do not understand any of this. Michael is my enemy."

"Well, now, I would not call him that, Emily. At the very least, he is merely a person you would rather not associate with."

"Fine, then. Perhaps enemy is overstating it a bit, but the point remains the same. How does one go from hating a man—all right, disliking him intensely," she added at Lily's disapproving look, "to wanting to kiss him? It does not make any sense."

"Love never does."

Emily bounced up from her chair. "I never said I was in love, Lily. I only said I wanted to kiss him." She clamped her hand over her mouth. "Dear me," she said behind her fingers. "I sound so shameless!"

Lily chuckled weakly. "On the contrary, Emily. You sound human. Have you talked to Michael about this?"

Emily removed her hand from her mouth and let it fall to her side. "Heavens, no. I could not possibly bring this up to him. Not only would it be embarrassing, it would provide him more fodder to make fun of me."

With a compassionate expression, Lily held out her hand. "Come here, darling," she said. When Emily slid her hand in Lily's, Lily drew her closer. "You have to believe me when I say this . . . the last thing Michael wants to do is hurt you."

The intensity of Lily's tone gave Emily pause. "How do you know?"

Lily squeezed Emily's hand. "I just do. We both realize Michael is, shall we say, an odd duck. But he isn't a bad person. And if you are able to see beneath his exterior and be attracted to him, then good for you." As if saying so many words had exhausted her, Lily leaned back against the sofa and closed her eyes.

Emily released her hand. Guilt threaded through her once again as she looked at her sister-in-law. Her complexion seemed to take on a grayish tinge, and she looked fatigued in the extreme. Instead of going on about herself, Emily should have been paying more attention to Lily's health. Pushing her selfishness aside, she kneeled down beside her. "Lily, are you all right?"

Lily nodded, but kept her eyes closed. "I am fine, truly. Simply tired. Sometimes it just comes over me, and all I want to do is sleep." Her lids opened to small slits. "I am sorry, Emily. I do not want to cut our conversation short."

"There is nothing to be sorry about, Lily. I understand." She patted her friend's arm and stood. "I will leave you be. Thank you for listening."

"My pleasure."

Emily made her way to the door. As she turned the knob, Lily called to her. "Emily, if you see Colin, reassure him I am right as rain. He does worry about me so."

"I will," Emily said, but cast a worried glance at Lily.

For all the woman's protestations, she didn't look right as rain at all. But Emily had no experience with pregnancy. Perhaps Lily's weakness and fatigue were to be expected.

Closing the door quietly behind her, Emily went back to her room. She slipped out of her dress and donned her nightclothes, then inserted herself between the cool sheets. She thought about what Lily had said, about seeing beneath Michael's irritating surface. Is that what had happened during those few moments at the picnic? There was also Lily's insistence that Michael didn't want to hurt her. If that was the case, then why did he insist on slinging verbal arrows at her?

Would she ever figure out the enigma that was Michael Balcarris? Somehow she doubted she ever would.

Chapter Fifteen

Somehow Michael had to figure out how to stay away from Emily.

He'd managed to avoid her for the rest of the day yesterday after leaving the picnic. He knew he should have helped her to her feet after he unceremoniously dumped her on the ground, but he had been so intent on getting away from her that he'd left her to her own devices. He knew if he had touched her again he might not have let her go. That would have been a big mistake.

But by far his biggest mistake had been going on the picnic in the first place. If he hadn't, then he wouldn't have given in to chasing her, he wouldn't have tripped, he wouldn't have pulled her on top of him, and he wouldn't have almost kissed her.

He lay in his bed and stared at the ceiling. It was morning, but he wasn't in any hurry to go downstairs and break his fast. He might run into her, and he wasn't ready for that. He shouldn't even be here in Yorkshire. If he had been thinking clearly, he would have sent a missive to Colin informing him of Pembrooke's intended duplicity. Then he would be a safe distance from Emily, which was exactly where he should be. Instead, he had been so filled with the desire to see her that he had lost all common sense.

In actuality, there was only one thing left for him to do—return to London. He had done his duty. He had already told Colin about Pembrooke. Colin was rightly outraged, but he was also distracted with concern for his wife, since Lily seemed to be getting weaker in her pregnancy rather than stronger. Thus, Michael had felt it necessary to warn Emily himself, and he had fulfilled that obligation yesterday, even though she didn't seem to take him seriously. However, that wasn't his problem anymore. What he needed to do was depart from Leton House, then come back in a couple of weeks and pick up his mother. What happened after he left was no longer his concern.

He flipped over onto his side and cradled a pillow. Closing his eyes, he couldn't keep the sweet moment of holding Emily in his arms at bay. She had been so soft, so pliable in his arms. He hadn't wanted to let her go. As much of a mistake as that had been, a part of him was glad it happened, for he had never experienced such a wonderful few seconds in his life. Another part of him wished that he could have given in to his impulses and kissed her right then and there. Maybe that was all he needed to do to get her out of his system. But he was only fooling himself, knowing full well that if he had started kissing her, he probably would never stop. Maintaining his will power had been the hardest thing he'd ever had to do.

He had to give her credit. It had been quite clever and amusing, leading him on a merry chase like that. So very much Emily. And he did enjoy it in the extreme. Emily had been right about one thing—he hadn't had fun in a long time. His life had been so consumed by work, by keeping up his disguise, by keeping his feelings and emotions bottled up that he never indulged in anything remotely pleasant. Yesterday she had given him a gift—a few moments of unadulterated pleasure.

But now it all had to come to an end. He forced himself to roll out of bed, found his case, and started packing. Thirty minutes later he was dressed and ready to leave. Taking his case, he went downstairs, set the luggage by the door, and went to find Colin.

Michael had assumed his friend was in the dining room having breakfast, and his assumption proved correct. Colin had just plopped a dollop of cream on a berry tart when Michael entered. Lily was to his right, nibbling on a plain scone, forcing down the bites. Her complexion had a grayish tinge to it. Michael felt a stab of pity, for she looked quite frail and rather miserable. "May I have a word with you, Colin?" he asked.

"Certainly." Colin removed his napkin, leaned over, and kissed Lily on the cheek. "I will be right back, love," he said, rising from his chair. "Please, finish the scone."

"I will try," she responded wearily, but set the scone down on her plate.

"She is not eating enough," Colin told Michael when they were out of the room. Worry lines creased his forehead. "I am truly concerned about her."

"Have you sent for the physician?"

"Not yet. She insists she is fine, just tired. She said her mother went through the same thing when she was pregnant. But Lily has always been so thin. I cannot see how her lack of appetite is good for the baby."

"You should trust her instincts, Colin."

"I have been, but if she does not improve soon, I will fetch someone myself." He looked at Michael. "I am sorry, I got sidetracked. What did you want to speak to me about?"

"I have to return to London."

Colin's eyebrows lifted. "Has something happened?"

"In a certain respect, yes. I cannot go into details, but I must depart at once."

"By all means. I am glad you were able to stay a short while."

"I would like to leave Mother here, if that is agreeable. She is enjoying herself immensely, and I hate to cut her visit short."

"She is welcome to stay as long as she likes. The rest of the summer, if she so chooses."

"Thank you for your hospitality. I will let her know that I am leaving."

"You are leaving? Why?"

Michael turned around to see Emily standing behind

him. She looked especially pretty this morning in a light green day dress, a circlet of pearls draped around her neck. His gaze automatically went to her rosy lips. Quickly he caught himself and looked away.

"Why are you leaving?" she repeated, walking toward him. "You only just got here."

"Do not be so nosy, Emily," Colin interjected, moving to stand in between them. "Michael can come and go as he pleases. He does not have to explain himself to you."

"And you do not have to insinuate yourself in our conversation."

"I believe Michael and I were having a conversation first before you so rudely interrupted."

Michael might have regarded the sibling squabble with a measure of amusement if he weren't in such a hurry to leave, and if Emily wasn't so devastatingly tempting to him. He shifted on his feet, trying to stem his impatience with them both.

"Never mind, Colin. I don't have the time or inclination to argue with you." She peered around her brother's arm and looked at Michael, then looked back at Colin. "Besides, I was on my way to tell you that I heard from Charles."

"Pembrooke?"

"Do I know any other Charles?" Emily said snippily. "He sent word this morning that he is on his way to visit."

"You must send word back that he can't," Colin commanded.

Emily's eyes widened. "What?"

"Mr. Pembrooke is not welcome here. Not now, and not ever."

"Why not? He was welcome back in London."

"That was before I found out what his true intentions were." Colin glanced over his shoulder and looked at Michael.

Emily frowned. "I see you have been listening to *him*." She pointed at Michael.

Colin stepped away. "Again, Emily, I will remind you that I do not have to explain myself either. I do not want you entertaining Mr. Pembrooke again. He is not a proper suitor."

"This is preposterous! You cannot send a man away on the basis of what Michael says."

"Yes, I can."

"Has he offered you any proof?"

"Emily, this is not up for debate, discussion, or dispute."

"Arghh!" Emily glared at Colin, then at Michael, then back at Colin again. "You two are the most exasperating individuals I have ever met." She pointed her finger at Colin. "You continually order me around like I am a child of three and incapable of understanding anything."

"Perhaps if your words and actions were not so childish, you would be treated differently," Colin muttered.

Emily ignored him. She was in mid-rant now and wasn't about to be derailed. "And you," she said, shaking her index finger at Michael, "you are the worst offender. First you call me sweetheart—"

"Wait—what?" Colin said, his expression changing from annoyance to bewilderment.

"Then you almost kissed me—"

"Hold on!" Colin turned to Michael. "You kissed my sister?"

"Almost," Emily corrected in a high voice.

Michael's head spun as he tried to grasp that not only did Emily practically ruin her reputation by implying that she and he were involved in an impropriety, but that somehow he had to come up with a way to fix her blunder. If she had been thinking clearly, which obviously she was not, she would have realized that she had just created a serious problem for herself. And for him. For both of them.

"Michael?" Colin said, glowering. "I am waiting for an explanation."

Michael looked at Emily, whose ire had finally seemed to cool. Consequently, she seemed to finally comprehend what her thoughtless words had done. She clamped her hand over her mouth, her blue eyes wide and pleading. *Fix this.*

"Well, now, Colin," he started. "It wasn't, ah, quite like that."

"Did you kiss my sister or not?"

"*Colin!*"

Lily's shriek echoed through the hallway, making them all jump. Their argument forgotten, Colin, Michael, and Emily ran to the dining room. Michael reeled in horror at the sight of Lily on the floor, clutching her belly in what appeared to be absolute agony.

Colin knelt by her side. "Darling! Oh, darling, what is it?"

"The . . . baby," she said in a strangled voice. She cried out as a wave of pain took over, causing her to curl up in a ball, both arms wrapped around her stomach. A patch of crimson blood was visible on her skirt.

"I will fetch the physician," Michael cried out before he dashed out of the room. He skidded to a halt in front of Emily, who was standing in front of the doorway. Her face had drained completely of color, and she stood as motionless as a statue. He placed both his hands on her arms and shook her firmly. "Get your mother, Emily," he said. "I will be back with the doctor as soon as I can."

She looked up at him, tears in her eyes. "She is losing the baby," she whispered thickly.

She looked lost, terrified. Michael ached to hold her and comfort her, to let her know everything would be all right. But they had no time to lose. "Don't say that!" He gripped her a little harder. "Fetch your mother. Now!"

She nodded, then turned and ran out of the room. Michael raced to the nearest town to locate Dr. Colgan, praying the entire way.

Chapter Sixteen

Emily had never been so terrified in her life. Fortunately, her mother and Ruby Balcarris were the epitome of calm during the increasingly perilous storm whirling around them. When she told both women what was happening to Lily, they took charge immediately and instructed Colin to carry her to Elizabeth's room, which was on the first floor.

Colin had laid his wife carefully on the soft feather bed, brushing damp strands of her hair back from her forehead. Emily had never seen her brother so gentle or so stricken. Lily's eyes remained closed, her breathing shallow. Elizabeth had directed Emily to retrieve some clean cloths. When she brought them back, her mother tucked them beneath Lily's skirt.

"Where's the bloody doctor?" Colin raged.

"Colin! That won't do." Elizabeth's voice was quiet,

but forceful. "If you cannot be composed for your wife, then you will have to leave."

Colin nodded contritely. "Sorry, love," he said, brushing the back of his hand down Lily's cheek.

"No, I am the one who is sorry," Lily said, her cheeks moist with tears. "I am sorry . . . I couldn't keep our baby."

"Shhh." Colin knelt at the side of the bed and laid his forehead on Lily's chest for a brief moment. "Do not speak of such things." He lifted his head. "Our baby is strong, darling. You are strong." He kissed her forehead, his lips lingering against her damp brow for a long moment before he pulled back to look into her eyes again. "This is nothing, just a little inconvenience that will quickly be dispensed with. Everything will be right as rain soon enough. I promise you that."

Emily watched helplessly as her mother and Ruby took care of Lily while her brother desperately tried to comfort his wife. Colin stayed by her bedside, whispering encouragement, stroking her hand, speaking words of love close to her ear. Ruby wet one of the cloths with cool water and put it on Lily's sweat-beaded brow.

Emily's fingers twisted together until spikes of pain traveled to her wrists. Lily simply couldn't lose the baby. It was inconceivable. She would be devastated if she did. They all would be.

It simply could not happen. She refused to entertain the thought.

Moments later, a slender, gray-haired man with a slightly stooped back entered the room. Emily remembered him as Dr. Colgan, the physician who had treated her head injury. Immediately he began clearing the room.

"Too many people in here!" he announced, making a shooing motion with his hands. "You all must leave now. Especially you." He pointed to Colin, who continued to cling to Lily's hand.

"I am not going anywhere!" Colin barked. "This is my wife. My baby—"

"And if you want your baby to live you need to let me do my job."

Reluctantly, Colin released Lily's hand. He kissed her white lips. "I will be right outside, sweetheart." Rising, he took one last look at her before heading out the door.

Ruby and Elizabeth moved to follow Colin. But Dr. Colgan put his hand on Elizabeth's arm. "Not you. You can stay. She might need you."

Elizabeth nodded, then returned to Lily's bedside.

Emily followed Ruby and Colin to the library, which adjoined Elizabeth's room. Ruby took Colin's hand and patted it gently. "She will be fine, dear. Lily is in good hands. Dr. Colgan delivered you, if I remember correctly."

Her words didn't seem to give Colin much comfort. He pulled back from her and walked to the window, then stared outside. Emily started to go to him, but Ruby shook her head. It was clear he wanted to be alone.

Emily turned away from her brother and started to pace. It was all she could think of doing. Never had she felt so frightened and helpless. When Lily suddenly cried out in pain, Emily froze. Colin turned from the window and cursed. Then Michael walked in.

Emily just stood there, looking at him. He appeared wind-blown, his clothing all askew, as if he had rode as fast as his horse could carry him. Gone was his arrogant expression, his snooty demeanor. Instead she saw concern and genuine worry etched on his face. She watched as he crossed the room and went to Colin. Standing by her brother's side, he said a few words to him in a low voice, touched him on the shoulder, then he walked away.

Emily met his gaze again. This time she saw something more than apprehension. This time she saw emptiness. She recognized it immediately, because she felt it herself.

Without thinking, she walked toward him. When she reached him, she pressed her face against his chest, put her arms around his waist, and sobbed, releasing all her fear for Lily and her baby into Michael's strong body. After a moment's hesitation, she felt his arm around her back, then his hand smoothing her hair.

They didn't say anything. They merely held on to each other, drawing strength from their embrace. Emily didn't try to understand how she could gain so much comfort, so much security from being wrapped in Michael's arms. But she did. Feeling his heart beat beneath her cheek, sensing the light strokes of his hand against her hair, it seemed that everything would be all right after all. But it didn't completely take away the guilt that assaulted her. "I should have known something was wrong," she said against Michael's chest.

Michael's hand stilled on her hair. "You cannot blame yourself for this, Emily."

"No, you do not understand." Emily pulled away from him. "I talked to her last night about . . ." she almost admitted that he had been the subject of the conversation, but she didn't want to venture into that territory. Not now, and especially not with him. "We were talking last night and she seemed so pale . . . so tired."

"Lily has had a difficult time throughout the pregnancy. None of us could have known this would happen." He touched her cheek. "You and your brother," he said softly, running his finger down her cheek, "both so wracked with guilt over something that isn't your fault. Lily's lucky to be so loved."

Emily saw a fleeting look of sadness in his eyes. It was an expression she wasn't used to seeing from him. He had surprised her more than once in the past few days. His changing expressions and behavior confused her, but not nearly as much as her own feelings did. She had hated him for so long, yet at that moment, as he gave her comfort, she couldn't imagine hating him ever again. Instead, she never wanted him to let her go.

Dr. Colgan suddenly appeared in the doorway, clearing his throat. Emily spun around but stayed close to Michael. The doctor's expression was inscrutable. Colin turned from the window and rushed toward him. "My wife . . . the baby?" he said, his voice rising with every syllable.

"Both are doing fine." Dr. Colgan calmly rolled down one of his sleeves, as if he had just finished having tea with the regent instead of saving two precious lives.

"Thank God," Colin said, grasping both sides of his head with his hands.

Emily silently echoed her brother's relief. She slumped against Michael, his arm securely around her waist.

"However, this incident serves as a warning," Dr. Colgan continued. "I must insist Lady Chesreton remain confined for the rest of her pregnancy. She is very weak and suffering from poor nutrition. I already explained to her that she must stay in bed as much as possible if she wants to deliver a healthy baby."

"Done," Colin announced, his tone brooking no argument. "How long must she stay confined?"

"At least three more months. She must also eat more. She is far too thin."

"I will make sure she stuffs herself at every meal."

Dr. Colgan chuckled as he buttoned the cuff of his sleeve. "I would not go that far, lad. You do not want her to be too big. Then she might have problems with the delivery."

As he continued to give Colin instructions regarding Lily's care, Emily was acutely aware that Michael still had his arm around her waist. She wondered if he even realized it. She could have stepped away. She probably should have stepped away, but she didn't. She still needed him, and she suspected he might have needed her too.

"Can I go see her?" Colin asked.

"Of course. But only you, for right now. She is exhausted, poor thing."

Colin dashed out of the room with the physician following behind. That left Emily and Michael alone.

As if he had come to his senses, he suddenly dropped his arm from her side and moved out of her range. He slicked back his rumpled hair, then tightened his cravat. Clearing his throat, he said, "I am glad she and the babe are all right."

Emily nodded. She couldn't say anything else, she could only stare at him. It amazed her that he could change his deportment so quickly. One moment he was embracing her tenderly, the next he was acting as if she were a stranger suffering from the plague. The familiar feeling of frustration started to rise within her. Why did he always have to act so oddly? He continually kept her off balance, and she didn't like that. Not one whit.

"Now that the crisis has passed," he said, "I will take my leave now. I must return to London."

"What? You are still planning to go?" Frustration aside, she realized she couldn't let him go. Not now. Not when she had so many questions that needed answering. Not when she wanted to feel his arms around her again. It didn't matter that she had loathed him for so many years. In the past two days she had seen glimpses of the man she had been infatuated with when she was younger. The man who had rescued her from a tree . . . from a fall off a horse . . . from diving into despair over the possible loss of a child.

Her mother had been right. Michael was her hero.

"Please, Michael," she whispered, stepping toward him. "Please . . . stay."

Torture. Sheer torture.

That was what his life had become. As Michael stood in the drawing room trying to make his feet carry him out of Leton House, all he could think about was how torturous it was to be in Emily's presence and to hear the pleading in her voice as she asked him to stay. Once again he had gotten a tiny taste of what it would be like to be with her. He had drawn strength from her during Lily's terrible ordeal. The Dymoke's weren't the only ones who would have been distraught over the loss of Lily and Colin's baby. He had tasted the fear and despair as acutely as if it had been his own niece or nephew at risk. It had been a horrible time of touch and go, but he and Emily had gotten each other through it. How could he walk out the door and leave that behind? How could he leave her at all? Especially when, for the first time ever, she actually wanted him to stay?

But he had to go. As always, he had to forcefully convince himself there was no future for them. That she deserved more than what he could offer her. That he had sworn himself to the crown and had a duty to fulfill. One he couldn't turn his back on.

Yet his mental reasoning sounded hollow. Unconvincing. Untenable. Especially when she was standing in front of him, her gaze filled with a myriad of emotions that tugged at his soul. Confusion. Frustration. Longing.

It was the longing that nearly did him in.

"Michael," she whispered his name. "You do not have to go."

"Yes. I do."

"Please." She moved closer to him. "Don't leave."

"Em—Miss Dymoke." He fought to maintain his composure. His hand ached to hold his quizzing glass. It was his prop, his safety net. The one thing he could hide behind. But it was packed in his case. Now he had nothing. Never had he felt more vulnerable.

"Do not leave," she repeated, "before we have a chance to talk. We do need to talk—don't we?"

It wasn't really a question. It was more a statement of fact. He knew they couldn't go on like this. Too much had happened between them. He had let his guard down too many times, had given in to his emotions too much. He had to talk to her, to say something that would cause her to hate him again. Then things would be the way they were, and the way they should be, with her loathing him and him still wanting her.

A torturous circle.

But what could he say to her? How could he hurt her once again? He'd done it so many times before, with sharply edged words and slicing glances. Over and over he had caused her aggravation instead of joy. And he had done it on purpose. It had been a necessary evil.

But that was before he had experienced the bliss of holding her. To have her cling to him as if he were her lifeline. To draw as much comfort from her as she received from him. Yet despite all of this, despite everything that had transpired, somehow he had to find the strength to kill what had started to grow between them.

"Miss Dymoke," he said again, trying not to choke on her name. "You are, indeed, correct. We must talk. Then afterward, I absolutely have to leave for London."

Emily took a deep breath. "Fair enough."

"Miss Dymoke?"

Michael and Emily turned to see Estelle standing in the doorway.

"There is someone here to see you, Miss Dymoke. A Mr. Charles Pembrooke? He said you were expecting him."

Chapter Seventeen

Emily could not think of a single person who possessed worse timing than Charles Pembrooke. He was the last person on earth she wanted to see at the moment. Irritation rose within her, and for once Michael hadn't caused it.

"Shall I let him in, Miss Dymoke?" Estelle stood there, her hands nervously fingering the edges of her apron. The afternoon's events had taken a toll on her as well. Everyone in the house had been concerned about Lily and the baby.

Emily wasn't sure what to do, but she did know it wasn't fair to keep Charles waiting. She remembered what her brother had said about Charles not being welcomed at Leton House. She still didn't understand why, especially since her brother seemed to be taking

Michael's word for it. Once thing for certain, she had to sort everything out, and she couldn't do it by sending Charles away. "Yes," Emily finally answered.

"No," Michael said at the same time.

Estelle furrowed her brows, looking from Emily to Michael then back to Emily again. "I beg your pardon?"

"Send him home," Michael ordered.

She turned to him. "Yes, my lord."

"Wait!" Emily called to Estelle. She stepped around Michael. "Tell him I will be there in a moment."

Estelle looked from Michael to Emily again, obviously unsure whose directive she should follow. Emily quickly went to her. "Estelle, allow Lord Hathery and I a few minutes, please." At Estelle's dubious expression, Emily said, "I promise to keep the door open. Mama won't mind, as Michael is a family friend."

"All right, miss. I will tell Mr. Pembrooke to wait outside."

"Thank you."

After Estelle departed, Emily turned to Michael. "Will you explain to me why you and my brother do not want me to see Charles?"

"I already told you. Charles is not to be trusted." Michael offered no further explanation than that.

Emily could feel her aggravation increasing exponentially, but instead of giving into it, she kept it in check. After this morning's events, she was far too tired to give in to her anger, especially knowing it wouldn't get her anywhere. "I believe I deserve a more tangible reason than that, Michael. Or at least some proof that he is after my money."

"Then you should take the issue up with Colin." Michael straightened his cravat for what seemed the umpteenth time, almost as if it were a nervous habit, a habit Emily hadn't noticed before.

"If you will not give me a valid reason for sending Charles back to London," she said, "especially after he's gone through the trouble of making the trip here, then I have no choice but to allow him to come in."

Michael's expression suddenly changed to one of warning. "Trust me. You do not want to do that."

"Trust you?" She let out a bitter laugh. "You won't be honest with me about anything and you want me to trust you?"

"When have I not been honest?"

"Ever since you arrived." Truly, she'd had enough of his nonsense. If he insisted on speaking in riddles, then he could bloody well do that. She, however, no longer wanted to work so hard to understand him. "Go back to London, Michael," she said wearily.

"Miss—"

"Please. Just . . . leave." She walked past him and headed for the front door. "Charles is waiting. At least he is forthright about his intentions and his feelings. With him, I do not have to play guessing games." Turning on her heel, she left the room, hoping Michael would follow. Or at least protest her departure. When he didn't, hollow emptiness seeped inside her soul.

*   *   *

"Botheration!" Michael said to the empty library after Emily's departure. He couldn't very well leave now, not with Pembrooke's arrival, and certainly not with the Dymoke family as vulnerable as it was. Colin would be consumed with caring for Lily, so much so that he could not be expected to deal with Pembrooke himself. And Emily was already hurt and confused, thanks to him. She would be doubly susceptible to whatever plan Pembrooke had cooked up.

There was only one thing Michael could do. He had to stay here and watch out for the family. For Emily in particular. All while keeping his distance and restraining his emotions.

In other words, life as usual.

He left the library and walked into the foyer just as Emily was letting Charles in.

The man took off his hat and gave Emily a deep bow. "You are a sight for this weary traveler's eyes, Miss Dymoke." He took her hand and kissed the top of it. When he finished he turned to Michael. "Lord Hathery, what a surprise. I had not expected to see you here."

"He was just leaving," Emily said, giving Michael a pointed look. "Weren't you, Lord Hathery?"

"Actually, I decided to extend my stay." He bent down to pick up his case.

Emily looked at him with surprise. And exasperation. "I thought you had pressing business in London?"

"It can wait for an extra day. Or two." He turned to Pembrooke. "How is our fine city?

"The same as always. Which is why I am glad to be in the country."

"Indeed." Both men kept their gaze squarely on one another until Emily stepped between them.

"Charles, I will have your things brought up to one of the guest rooms upstairs." She turned to Michael. "You know where you can go."

Ouch. Michael had to acknowledge the poisoned sting of her comeback. He didn't blame her for being snippy with him, of course. At this point he was beyond irritated with himself, so he could only imagine how she felt.

Then again, he didn't have to imagine it. Without a word or passing glance in Michael's direction, Emily escorted Charles further into the house. "Allow me to show you around Leton House," she said with exaggerated sweetness.

"I would be honored," Charles replied.

They left Michael alone in the foyer. He picked up his case and headed upstairs to quickly unpack. Charles wouldn't get Emily alone so easily, and he wouldn't get rid of Michael at all. Michael would make sure of that.

"Forgive me for saying so, Miss Dymoke, but have I come at a bad time?"

Emily looked at Charles. They were sitting in the garden, in full view of all the windows in the house. She knew her mother and Ruby were upstairs keeping an eye on her and Charles, but other than that they were alone. She had already given him a succinct tour of the house and grounds, and she was too tired to do much more.

But that didn't mean she should be rude to Charles. It wasn't his fault that he had shown up at such an inopportune time. In actuality, her entire summer holiday seemed to have been doomed from the start. It scared her to think that anything else horrible might happen. What that could possibly be she couldn't fathom, considering the near tragedy they had all experienced earlier in the day. "We did have a bit of a scare this morning," she said, downplaying the nightmare of Lily's near-miscarriage. "But things are back to normal now."

"I see." He didn't ask her to elaborate, and for that she was glad. If he had, where would she have begun? With her accident? Her near-kiss with Michael? Lily's and Colin's brush with devastation? Or her growing and inexplicable romantic feelings for a man she could hardly stand to be around most of the time? One thing she did know for sure—she didn't want to revisit any of that. Particularly with Charles. He would think her truly mad if she did.

She regarded him for a moment, trying to discern some sign from him that he was the gold digger Michael and Colin accused him of being. But she had a hard time believing their suspicions. He came across as so genuine, so sincere . . . she could hardly believe Michael and Colin's accusations were true. She doubted them even more since neither man was willing to offer any proof that Charles's intentions were less than authentic. Unbidden, a lump formed in her throat. Was it so hard for them to believe that a man could love her for her? That he could look beyond the size of her hips and the fullness of her body and want her anyway?

Maybe that was the reason why Michael always pulled away from her when they had gotten close. She reviewed the past couple days' events, and realized, to her horror, that she had possibly read much more than what was there. Perhaps, deep down, she had always harbored romantic notions of Michael, despite the antagonistic nature of their relationship over the years. That would explain her desperation to see a romantic interest in her that didn't exist.

Her cheeks flamed at the thought. Michael must believe her a complete lunatic. No wonder he wanted to get away from her so desperately.

Charles moved a little closer to her on the stone bench. "Are you sure your brother doesn't mind that I am here?" he asked, breaking into her thoughts.

Emily swallowed her pain and forced herself to focus on Charles. At least she hadn't embarrassed herself in front of him—not yet, anyway. One thing she certainly couldn't do was tell him that Colin wanted him far, far away from Leton House. If she told him the truth, he would definitely want elaboration on that. Instead, she chose to be vague and to twist the truth a bit. "He is very busy with Lily right now. I do not think he will be the least bit concerned about your presence."

"That is a relief." He clasped his hat in his hands. "I must admit, I was surprised to see Lord Hathery here."

"He and his mother came for a visit," she said quietly.

"Is that customary?"

"No, not usually. I think Lady Hathery wanted to get out of London for a while." Now that she thought about it, she didn't actually know why Michael and his mother had shown up out of the blue. Especially only a day after she and her family had left. If Ruby had wanted to escape from London, why didn't they go to their own country house in the dales? Or anywhere else, for that matter? Why here?

Unless it had to do with Michael warning her about Charles. But that didn't make sense either. Why would he go to such trouble to come all the way from London when he could have just sent her brother a letter? Dear Lord, she was so very, very confused.

"Emily? Is everything all right? You've become very quiet all of the sudden."

Charles's voice drew her out of her thoughts. "I am sorry. I did not mean to be. It has been a very trying day."

"That is quite all right. If you are not interested in talking, we don't have to. I'll be happy to sit here and keep you company." He looked at her and smiled.

Really, she should have had some reaction to his grin and his gallantry. He had a handsome countenance, and his smile only accentuated it. But she remained unmoved. She waited for her heart to flip or her stomach to flutter, or at the very least her mouth to go dry. She experienced none of these things in Charles presence.

But she had experienced every one of them in Michael's. Blast, she was hopeless. Despite her self-talk about there being nothing between her and Michael, for some reason she couldn't accept it. There was also nothing she could do about it either.

"No," she said suddenly, changing her mind in an attempt to get Michael out of it. "I would like very much to talk." At least when she was talking she could focus more on Charles and less on Michael.

Charles glanced up at the windows and scooted a little closer to her once again. "I am glad to hear that. I could not wait to get here to see you. I have something very important to speak to you about."

Emily drew back as a sense of foreboding overwhelmed her. Lately any time a man said he had something to tell her, it usually ended up in an argument. Or a disaster. She wasn't in the mood for either one. "You do?" she managed to ask.

"Yes. And I believe now is as good a time as ever. I know we have not known each other that long, but I have come to feel that you and I are well suited. Keeping that in mind, I wanted to ask you to—"

"Lovely evening for a stroll in the garden, don't you think?"

Emily looked up to see Michael peering down at her and Charles through that blasted quizzing glass of his. She absolutely abhorred that thing. "Michael," she greeted him through gritted teeth.

"Miss Dymoke. Mr. Pembrooke. May I join you?"

"No—" Charles started.

"Why, thank you." Michael sat down on the bench opposite the two of them. He crossed one leg over the other, allowing the free leg to swing back and forth.

Emily found her attention drawn to his stockings, which were impeccably white. They also encased very muscular calves, another aspect of Michael she hadn't noticed before.

This time, her stomach did flutter in quite a pleasant and warm way.

"Lord Hathery," Charles said, sounding more than a little perturbed that he and Emily's dialogue had been intruded upon, "as much as we would enjoy your company, Miss Dymoke and I were in the middle of a very important conversation."

"You were? Oh, then a thousand pardons for interrupting." Despite his words, he made no move to get up. "Carry on, please."

"I would prefer to carry on privately." Charles gave Michael a black look.

"Oh, don't mind me. Pretend I am not here. I am sure whatever you have to say to Miss Dymoke is of no import to me anyway."

Emily's eyes narrowed. "Michael, stop being exasperating."

"*Moi?* Exasperating? Perish the thought." He toyed with the feather on the end of his quizzing glass, but remained firmly seated on the stone bench, as if he were stuck there by some invisible glue.

"Perhaps there is another place where we can talk?" Charles suggested, looking at Emily rather desperately.

"There are dozens of places you could go to," Michael said. "Some allow more privacy than others. There is the vegetable garden on the other side of the house. But the beehive is there, so I would not recommend it. The pests never like it when their habitat is disturbed. Then there are the stables. However the aroma near the building can be quite pungent. Not exactly suitable for a lady of Miss Dymoke's caliber. Then there is the—"

"Enough!" Charles popped up from his seat. "I don't know what game you are playing, Lord Hathery, but I am done with it. You are being rude in the extreme, and I will not have you irritating Miss Dymoke."

Michael gave Charles one of his trademark blank looks, then turned to Emily. "Is it true, Miss Dymoke? Am I irritating you?"

Suddenly, Emily had the hysterical and inexplicable urge to laugh. She bit the inside of her lip, figuring if she elicited the merest hint of a chuckle Charles, in his current agitated state, would probably go round the bend. Emily felt fairly certain she was halfway round the bend herself. But that didn't take away from the fact that she understood exactly what Michael was doing.

He was having fun.

True, he was having a joke at the expense of poor Charles. Which really could be considered bad form, if she chose to look at it that way. She cast a sideways glance at Charles, who wasn't even trying to hide his anger from Michael. He was positively seething. Just the way she used to do when Michael yanked on her chain in almost the same way.

"Lord Hathery, I must ask that you depart our company at once!"

"But Miss Dymoke hasn't answered me." He turned

and looked at Charles. "I will tell you this, Mr. Pembrooke. If Miss Dymoke requests I take my leave, then I will do so without a moment's hesitation. I have put the ball in her court, so to speak."

Charles turned to Emily, an expectant look on his face. When she didn't answer right away, he said, "Emily?"

Weariness suddenly overcame her, replacing her earlier amusement. Suddenly it wasn't funny anymore. Instead, everything was becoming too much, and she felt like the rope in their personal tug of war. She didn't want to deal with Michael or Charles anymore. At least not tonight. "If you will both excuse me, I think I will retire early tonight. Feel free to enjoy each other's company. Mr. Pembrooke. Lord Hathery. Good night." With that she stood and left the garden, and both men, behind.

Michael and Pembrooke stared at each other. In actuality the other man was currently glaring at Michael as Michael tried to look impassive. It was difficult to do, considering he wanted to shake the man within an inch of his life.

He knew exactly why Pembrooke was furious with him. Michael had interrupted him at the precise moment he was going to propose to Emily. Michael's arrival hadn't been coincidental; he had waited by the garden entrance until Pembrooke had made his move. He took particular delight in thwarting the man's plans. He was ready to thwart them even further by telling Pembrooke to leave the premises. Although it was actually Colin's place to do so, this was one task Michael didn't mind doing on his friend's behalf.

Pembrooke's fists were clenched at his sides. He wasn't taking Michael's intrusion lightly. "The next time you see Miss Dymoke and I having a private conversation, I strongly suggest you leave us alone. Your presence tonight was unnecessary and exceedingly rude."

"I disagree, Mr. Pembrooke. As a close friend of the family, I am allowed to spend time in the garden when I wish. I daresay it is you who are the intruder."

"Hardly. Miss Dymoke was expecting me."

"Only after you manipulated your way into a visit." Michael suddenly realized there was something strange occurring during their conversation. As Pembrooke spoke, he kept glancing at the window upstairs. He had also slowly moved toward the back of the garden. Without realizing it, Michael had matched him step for step. The man had done a smash-up job of leading them away from the house. They were now in a more secluded part of the garden, away from the window's view.

"You would do well to mind your own business, Lord Hathery," Charles said, his voice taking on a sinister quality. They were now in the darker shadows of a cherry tree near the side edge of the garden. "Spying on others will only lead you to trouble. Possibly even death."

A cold sensation raced up and down Michael's spine. He could no longer see Pembrooke clearly now, as most of his body was obscured by the shadows. Michael cursed inwardly. He'd been an utter fool. If he hadn't let his passion for Emily get in the way of his rational thought, he would have noticed Pembrooke's intent early on. In fact, he should have realized it all along, not when it was too late.

Not when he had stepped right into the man's trap.

The sharp glint of steel caught his eye. It slashed through the darkness, aimed straight at him.

Chapter Eighteen

Emily had made it halfway across the front threshold of the house before she halted her steps. This wasn't right, and she knew it. She was running away from her problems instead of facing them head on. She had used her fatigue as an excuse to avoid an overdue confrontation with both Michael and Charles. Instead of settling everything between herself and the two men, she opted to spend another sleepless night tossing and turning and worrying about what she would say to them in the morning. That would have been more difficult than standing her ground and demanding some honest answers.

She didn't know what had precipitated it, but suddenly everything that had been muddled for so long became clear.

The time had come to settle things with Charles. It had been wrong of her to lead him on in the first place.

She had known from the beginning that there was nothing between them, and that there never would be, but she had allowed him to think that there was. Leading him on had been wrong.

She now realized that Gavin had been kind, not cruel, when he had been honest with her that day months ago. His rejection had hurt, but she could only imagine the pain she would be in now if he hadn't been truthful with her. Maybe Michael was right and Charles only wanted her money. But even if Charles didn't have the decency to be candid with her, she still had to be straightforward with him.

She also had to come to terms with Michael and the feelings she had developed for him. He infuriated her and intrigued her. He exasperated her and made her feel safe and protected. He had been there for her when she needed him, and he had pushed her away when she wanted him. It was as if he were two different people. She had to find out why.

She also had to tell him how she felt. Her attraction to Michael wasn't anything like her infatuation with Gavin. The emotions were deeper, more intense than she had ever experienced. And even if he didn't reciprocate her sentiment, she had to express it to him. She didn't know how he would respond to her honesty, but she was willing to take the risk.

Closing the front door, she turned and headed back around the house to the garden. When she reached the edge of it, she was taken aback by the quiet of the evening. She had expected to see the two men arguing with each other, as Charles had looked ready to come to blows with Michael when she left. Instead the stone benches were empty. Perhaps they had come to some kind of truce. She frowned as disappointment overcame her. She'd spent the last few minutes bolstering her courage and it was all for naught. Clarifying her thoughts and feelings was also all for naught. Of course the way her day had gone, she shouldn't have been surprised. Just one more conflict in the course of a very frustrating day.

Turning around, she was about to go back to the house when she saw some movement in the shadows. Squinting against the darkness, she made out the back of Michael's silver-gray jacket. She watched him abruptly jump backward, as if some kind of apparition had attacked him.

"Michael?" she called out as she neared the shadowed side of the garden. "Charles?"

"Emily, run!"

Michael's panicked command reached her ears. Before she could act in response, Charles suddenly appeared, holding something shiny in his hand. Emily breathed in sharply. The glistening tip of the weapon was pointed at Michael. Michael stepped back, his hands held out in front of him, palms facing Charles, warding off the assailant.

To her shock, Charles suddenly turned to her. "I wouldn't go anywhere if I were you," he said. He thrust his hand into his jacket pocket and pulled out a gun, pointing the shiny barrel at Emily.

"Charles?" she said, barely able to get his name past her lips. "For God's sake . . . what are you doing?"

"Pembrooke," Michael said. "Don't. It's me you want. Leave her alone."

"I cannot. She's too involved in this now." He moved closer to her, keeping the pistol aimed squarely at her chest.

Emily prayed she wouldn't pass out from fear. She could see Charles plainly now. He no longer resembled the gentleman who vied for her affections. Instead he appeared manic, as if he tottered on the edge of madness. He looked ready to shoot her at any moment.

"You said he wanted my money," she said to Michael, her voice rising to near hysterical volume. "You did not tell me he lost his mind."

"Don't say anything else, Emily," Michael cautioned, his tone forceful and deadly serious.

"Don't you think you should have mentioned it?" Emily asked, her voice verging on hysteria. "Did you think I would not have been interested in that little tidbit of information?"

"Emily, for once in your life, listen to me!"

"Give me one good reason why I should!"

"Quiet!" Charles barked. "Or I shall shut you up myself."

Emily slammed her lips together.

"Move," he ordered, gesturing at her with the gun. "Stand right next to him. That's it." He bobbed the gun barrel back and forth between Emily and Michael, his movements reminiscent of a child's game. "Now . . . I just have to decide who to kill first."

She felt Michael grasp her arm at the precise moment she began to sway. Dear heavens, she did not want to faint right then and there. Digging deep inside, she found her resolve and refused to lean against him. Anger had encroached on her fear. "If I die tonight I will never forgive you, Michael Balcarris."

"We can fight about this later," Michael said, his voice low in her ear. "Emily, he isn't joking around. That is a real gun he's holding, not a toy."

"I know, Michael. I am not stupid."

"Then listen to me. I assure you he will not hesitate to use it. You must do what he says." He gripped her arm harder, causing pain to radiate to her fingertips.

"Ouch! How dare you!"

"Don't you two ever stop bickering?" Charles asked impatiently. "You are worse than two children and just as tedious. I should put you both out of your misery right now."

"Pembrooke, don't be a fool," Michael said.

"I can assure you, Lord Hathery, I am not a fool."

"You will never get away with this."

"Yes, I will. All it takes is two shots and you will both be gone."

"My family is inside," Emily pointed out, unable to maintain her silence. Her body shook violently, but she couldn't just stand here and not try to talk him out of killing them. "They will hear you. They will alert the authorities."

"True, but by that time you will both be dead. At first they won't realize I took your lives. By the time they do, I will be long gone, headed back to France . . . and ready to collect my reward."

"Is that who sent you to kill me?" Michael asked. "The French government?"

"The government? Of course not. They are ineffectual twits. Besides, you flatter yourself. The government has more to concern itself with than you. I work independently. My benefactor prefers to remain anonymous, and I do not care who he is or what he stands for. As long as I do my job, he pays me well. And right now, my job is to exterminate you, Lord Hathery. Or should I say who you really are—Michael Balcarris, British spy?"

"A spy?" In her shock, Emily tried to comprehend what Charles had said. Suddenly everything made a mad sort of sense. His strange behavior. The long trips abroad. Now that she thought about it, the signs had always been there. He had been in disguise, and she had been too dense and too caught up in herself and her superficial perception of him to realize it.

She turned and looked at Michael. He kept his profile to her. It was set in stone. She had never seen him look so volatile. Or so strong. Even though he was being held at gunpoint, he seemed in complete control of the situation. There wasn't a shred of fear or doubt visible on his face.

"You are making a big mistake, Pembrooke. Surely your benefactor is not paying you to kill two people. Why take the risk?"

Charles gave Emily a lascivious look. "I consider her a bonus." Keeping the gun trained on her, he took a step forward. With his hand he touched her cheek, running his palm over her skin until he was cupping her chin.

"Why, Charles?" Emily whimpered, deeply afraid now. "Why are you doing this to me?"

"To get to him, of course. I am sorry, Emily, but it was never about you. When I saw you two arguing at the party that night, I knew I had found the perfect way to get to him. He is very protective of you. It was obvious to me that night. All I had to do was make you and him believe that I wanted you, and everything fell into place. I planted the seed in Michael that I was only pursuing you because of your money. As I suspected, he rushed to you, probably to warn you about my nefarious intentions."

He looked at Michael and sneered. "You were so predictable, Hathery, even though you thought you were being clever. I knew you were eavesdropping on me and the attendant at White's, just as I knew you would not allow Emily to be taken advantage of. I had expected much more of a challenge from you, considering your international reputation. Instead, it was like child's play. But as they say, every man has a weakness. Miss Emily Dymoke is clearly yours."

Charles then turned back to Emily and caressed her bottom lip with his thumb. "You are a pretty little thing. A tad too plump for my taste, and you can be quite petulant, but I could have gotten used to your more-deficient attributes. I will admit it was rather enjoyable pursuing you, Emily. If things had been different, we may have actually been able to make a go of it."

"Never," Emily spat.

He didn't appear the least bit ruffled by her response. "Well, then, as long as we both don't have any regrets." He gazed at her for a moment, tightening his grip on her face.

"Unhand her!" Michael said, lunging at Charles. But the click of the gun's cocking mechanism stopped him from moving further.

"Ready to say good-bye to her already?" Charles shook his head. "Again you surprise me, Hathery. I would have thought you would be more careful." He kept his gaze trained on Emily. "Did you know he was a spy? From your lack of response I can see that you did not. Perhaps he does not care as much for you as I thought if he did not think enough of you to tell you the truth about his life."

But Charles was wrong. She knew Michael cared for her. Everything Charles had said proved it. And most importantly, she knew it in her heart. Lily had told her to trust her heart, and she would do just that. It gave her courage to stand up to Charles. Jerking away from his grasp, she cried, "Michael cares for me, I know that now. He does not have to prove it you. He does not have to prove anything to you!"

Charles's gaze narrowed with displeasure. "You are quite bold for someone who is about to lose her life."

He lifted the gun and pointed it directly at her heart. "I am weary of this conversation. We have wasted enough time here. "Say good-bye to your lover, Miss Dymoke."

Emily froze, trickles of cold sweat sliding down her back. Black spots swam in front of her eyes as she gasped for air. But before she could catch her breath, Michael shoved Charles away, tackling him to the ground. The men slammed against the flagstones and rolled around as Michael tried to wrest the gun from Charles's grip. Two shots suddenly rang into the air.

"Michael!" Emily screamed.

Charles collapsed on top of Michael's body. Both men didn't move.

"Oh, God!" Emily ran toward them. As soon as she reached the men, Michael pushed Charles off of him. Charles rolled over onto his back. He remained completely still. Michael sat up, struggling for breath.

"Michael, oh, Michael," she said, putting her arms around him. When she realized that he had risked his life to save hers, she released him, and slapped him on the shoulder. Hard.

"What were you thinking! You could have been killed!" Then she looked at Charles, and felt the color drain from her face. "Is he dead?"

Carefully Michael moved closer to the man's inert body. He touched two fingers to his neck. "No. But he needs medical attention straight away."

The sound of running footsteps resounded in the darkness. "Emily!" Colin shouted as he dashed into the garden. He briefly surveyed the scene, then hurried over to his sister. "I came as soon as I heard the shots. What the bloody hell happened?"

"I will explain later," Michael said, his voice sounding raspy. "But Pembrooke has been shot. He is alive . . . yet he might not be for long."

"Dr. Colgan is going to start charging us double fees," Colin said without humor. "This will be his second visit today."

"How can you be so calm, Colin?" Emily said. "The man has been shot, for heavens sake!"

"He is not the only one." Michael opened his coat jacket.

Emily gasped. A crimson stain covered the left side of his waistcoat. His body started to shake. Immediately she drew him into her embrace, rubbing her hands along his arms in futility. Tears ran down her face and dripped onto his shoulder. "If you die tonight, Michael, I swear I will never forgive you."

"I believe I have heard that before," he replied weakly, looking up at her. He turned to Colin. "Hurry, mate." Then he collapsed in Emily's arms.

Chapter Nineteen

Michael lifted his eyelids, then closed them when bright light pierced his eyes. A few moments later he tried again, blinking as he adjusted to the light. He tried to move his left arm, then groaned in pain. This wasn't the first time he'd been shot, but it was probably the most serious wound he'd sustained. Glancing down at his chest, he could see it was bare except for a bandage wrapped around his upper torso and right shoulder. He licked his lips. They were dry. Blast, he was so thirsty.

He looked around the room, recognizing his surroundings. He was in the library of all places, in a makeshift bed on the settee. He almost laughed at the absurdity of it. After being shot, he couldn't have made it up the stairs. With Lily convalescing in Elizabeth's room, the library seemed an obvious place for him to recover. The way things were going, it wouldn't be long before Leton House in its entirety became an infirmary.

Taking a deep breath, he tried to sit up. He needed some tea or lemonade, even water would suffice at this point. Anything to quench his thirst. Grabbing the back of the settee, he used his good arm as leverage to get to a sitting position.

"What do you think you are doing?"

His head jerked at the sound of Emily's sharp reprimand. Without a word he dropped back on the couch. Her stormy tone matched the expression on her face. She wouldn't brook any argument from him. He thought it better to surrender than be defeated.

"Lie back down," she said, coming to him. She reached out and fluffed the pillow behind his head. He couldn't think of anyone else he'd rather have as his nursemaid, even though her bedside manner seemed to be lacking at the moment. "There. Are you more comfortable now?"

"Thirsty," he croaked.

"Let me get something for you to drink." She left the room, only to return shortly afterward with a tray laden with a pot of tea, teacups, and a plate of sandwiches. Behind her trailed Elizabeth and his mother. Emily set the food down while Ruby kissed his cheek and began to fret.

"Oh, darling, you had me so worried. To think that horrible man had planned to rob all of us blind. You were so brave to try to apprehend him."

Robbery? Michael had been shot, but he didn't think his mind had been affected. Pembrooke was an assassin, not a burglar. "I beg your pardon?"

"Colin explained everything. He said you and Emily had caught Mr. Pembrooke stealing some of her jewelry and he was trying to escape through the garden. Then he pulled a gun . . ." Ruby shuddered. "Fortunately Colin did not go into graphic detail. I do not think I could have taken that. He did say you were quite heroic in apprehending him." She clasped her hands together and steepled them under her chin. "I knew you were a special young man, Michael dear. I just had no idea you were so courageous. To think you risked your life to save Colin and Emily. I am so proud of you!"

Michael looked at Emily, who, incredibly, managed to remain impassive as she poured a cup of tea. He reminded himself to thank Colin for his quick thinking later. It wasn't a perfect cover story, but it served its purpose. His mother and Elizabeth didn't suspect anything, which was all that mattered. Although he didn't especially relish how his mother was treating him like a four-year-old child in front of Emily, he didn't dare say anything.

Emily handed him a cup of the tepid tea. Pulling a chair closer to the settee, she sat down next to him and helped him drink.

He gulped it down. "Thank you," he said, giving her back the cup. His voice sounded less scratchy now.

"We should let him rest, Ruby," Elizabeth said, standing next to her friend.

Ruby looked doubtful. "I do not want to leave him alone. What if he needs anything?"

"Emily will get it for him. I am sure she will take good care of him."

Michael thought he saw a knowing look exchange between Elizabeth and her daughter, but he wasn't positive.

Ruby, however, didn't seem convinced. "Michael? Would you like us to leave?"

"It might be best, Mother. I will probably just fall back asleep again. It would be dreadfully boring for you."

"Very well," Ruby said, finally agreeing. "I will do as you ask. But be assured, I will check on you in a couple of hours."

"I would not expect anything less."

When the ladies left, Michael turned to Emily. "A robbery? That was the best story Colin could come up with?"

"It was all *I* could think of."

Michael was impressed. He'd expected more from Colin because of his training, but for Emily to think so well under such pressure was quite a feat.

"I figured you did not want me telling Colin what really happened. I doubt he would have believed me anyway."

"Oh, you would be surprised. You should never underestimate your brother."

"Why do you say that?"

"Never mind." His cover was blown, but that didn't mean he needed to expose Colin. "What about Pembrooke? What happened to him?"

"He survived his wound. Dr. Colgan attended to him first. You insisted upon it, you stubborn man."

Michael vaguely recalled doing something of that sort, but his memory of what happened after he'd been shot was fuzzy at best. However, he absolutely remembered what had happened in the garden. Remorse nearly knocked the breath out of him. He had never wanted to put her in danger, and she had nearly been killed. "I had no idea what Pembrooke was truly up to. I should have, and it is my fault for not paying attention. I am sorry you had to go through such a horrible ordeal, Emily."

"I am not."

His eyes widened. "How can you say that? He assaulted you. He almost killed you—he *would* have killed you—"

"Had you not stopped him." She leaned forward and gazed at him closely. "Why didn't you tell me your secret, Michael?"

He sighed. "I could not, Emily. I could not tell anyone. I had sworn my oath to the crown, and I had to perform my duty. The disguise was necessary to alleviate suspicion. No one would ever accuse a vain, vacuous fop of being a spy."

She was listening to him, but with an impatient air. Waving her hand back and forth she said, "That is not what I meant." She reached for his hand and entwined her fingers in his. "What I want to know is . . . why didn't you tell me how you felt? Why didn't you tell me that you cared for me?"

All of the sudden his mouth went dry, and it wasn't because he was thirsty. He couldn't respond right away.

He didn't know how to. It was as if the touch of her soft hand against his had sent any coherent thoughts flying out of his head. For so long he had dreamed of this moment, of telling Emily that he loved her. Visions of such a scene had played in his mind over and over, had kept him up at night and had haunted his days. Now he had the opportunity to tell her what was in his heart. To confirm what she already suspected. Yet he couldn't form the words.

"I think I know why you never said anything." She released his hand and pulled away. "You didn't trust me enough to tell me either secret."

He shook his head. "That was not the reason," he insisted.

"No, it is all right, Michael. I understand now. I wouldn't have trusted myself either. Actually I wouldn't blame you if you never wanted to speak to me again." She swallowed, her blue eyes glistening. "I have been such an idiot. When you returned from Oxford I was so angry with you. You had changed, and not for the better. At least that was what I thought. But I never bothered to look past the surface, or to find out why you were so different. I never paid attention to what was in front of me all along."

Michael sat up as much as he could, wincing slightly as a sharp pain pierced his chest. Ignoring it, he turned and looked at her. "This is not your fault, Emily. Do not ever think that. I had to fool everybody, not just you. Even my own mother didn't know who I really was. She still doesn't."

"That must have been very difficult for you."

"It was. I mean it is. But not as difficult as . . ." He averted his gaze, still unable to expose what he had kept locked away in his heart for so long.

"As what?"

He looked into her eyes and remembered what Clewes had said about not letting Emily get away. She knew his secret now. She knew how he felt about her. But she didn't know everything.

He had to tell her. He had to do it now.

"Emily, I have been a spy for almost twelve years. I have traveled all over the world gathering secrets for the crown to use against its enemies. I have had to give up my friends, my family, my very identity. All of that has been a tremendous hardship." He took her hand in his. Her skin was so very soft, and he relished the feel of it against his palm. It took every fiber of his being not to press his lips against her fingers. "But none of it compares to how difficult it has been keeping my feelings for you hidden. I love you, Emily. I have loved you for years."

Tears fell down her face. "You have?"

"Yes. I have."

"But I have been so horrible to you!" She sniffed, wiping the moisture from her cheeks with her free hand. "How can you possibly love me?"

"I am not without blame. I knew exactly what to do and say to upset you."

"Why? Why would you do that if you loved me?"

"It was *because* I love you." He reached up and

brushed her tear-stained cheek with his thumb. "Don't you understand? I could not let you know how I felt. It was too dangerous. Even when I tried to protect you, I still put you in harm's way."

"Charles."

He nodded. "I had no idea what he was up to, Emily. You have to believe me. That is probably impossible after I have lied to you all these years. But if you do not believe anything else I have said to you, please understand this one thing. I would have never left London if I'd had any suspicion he was setting a trap."

She smiled, one of her tears settling in the corner of her mouth. "Oh, Michael, I do believe you. And it's not your fault, truly it isn't. I would not listen to you, remember? I didn't trust you or Colin. I let Charles into my house, into my life. I did not even care anything about him. I only defied you out of pride. I should have listened to you both. As it turned out, he was not interested in me at all."

"I am so sorry he hurt you, Emily."

"But he didn't. He didn't hurt me at all." She gripped his hand tightly. "You want to know why I came back to the garden, Michael? It was because I realized I never should have left. I was running away from both of you. I needed to tell him I wasn't interested in him romantically. And I needed to talk to you, to figure out what was going on between us."

His heart soared. Instead of blaming him, she was taking the blame on herself. Instead of attacking him, she was reaching out. Despite everything she was staying beside him, holding his hand as if she never wanted to let it go. He'd never loved her more than at that moment.

"Once Dr. Colgan had stabilized Charles's wound, Colin turned him over to the authorities. He never said who had paid him to assassinate you."

"He probably never will. He is a professional killer, Emily, and he will more than likely hang. If not for attempting our murders, then for the murders he committed in the past."

"You sound so sure," she said, sounding doubtful.

"This is not the first time someone has tried to take my life." At her gasp, he quickly reassured her. "I am not afraid of death, Emily. It has been a possibility ever since I started spying. But I am terrified of something happening to you. I could not bear it if it did."

"You were willing to die for me," she whispered. "How can I ever repay you for that?"

"You do not have to." He cupped her face in his hand. "I do not want any obligations between us, Emily. I told you the truth not because I want you in my debt, but because you deserve honesty. You deserve to know what I have been keeping from you all these years." He let his hand slip away from her. "I would understand if you wanted me to leave. Just say the word and I will go. No questions asked."

"Leave?" Emily couldn't believe what she was hearing. Without question Michael was the most vexing man she'd ever encountered. Even when he was being his real self, he managed to confound her completely.

"Michael, it is time for me to be honest with you. I don't understand why you're pushing me away again."

"I am not pushing you away."

"You are. You expect me to reject you without giving me a chance." She bit her bottom lip. "I have a secret of my own, by the way. One I have held longer than you've had yours."

His brows arched with curiosity. With his stubbly growth of beard, no-longer pinched facial expression, and genuine inquisitiveness sparking in his eyes, she found him incredibly gorgeous. Once again the flutter in her stomach returned. She loved how he made her feel.

"I had a crush on you when I was a girl," she blurted out, the warm emotions flowing through her, giving her the nudge she needed to reveal one of the more embarrassing skeletons occupying her closet. "I was devastated when you went away to Oxford, even though I knew you had to go."

"You were?" A smile twitched at the corners of his mouth. "Clever girl. I had no idea. It seems you are better at keeping secrets than I am."

She blushed. "Maybe so. But then you returned from school—"

"As a vainglorious peacock," he supplied.

"Yes. That is a good way to describe it. At first I was confused. You weren't the same Michael I adored from afar. Then I became upset. But before long I had to come to terms with the fact that you had changed so much, I did not know who you were any more. It was at that point I had to give up on my feelings for you."

Michael's expression grew serious. "Honestly, Emily, I had no clue. You never hinted at feeling anything for me but loathing."

She rolled her eyes. "Do not remind me." Then she smiled. "But now . . . now things are different."

He grinned back. "They certainly are." Then to her dismay, his smile faded. "But they are no less complicated."

Her heart stilled at the solemnity of his tone. "What do you mean?"

"I am still a spy, Emily. Charles Pembrooke figured out who I was. I am sure he will not be the last assassin to do so. I care for you too much to put you in that kind of danger."

She released his hand. "For goodness' sake, Michael! Would you let that be my decision?"

"But you do not understand the consequences."

"I think I do." She gestured to his bandages. "You weren't the only one held at gunpoint."

"My point exactly. Why would you put yourself through that again?"

"Because you're worth it, Michael. You are absolutely worth it."

He didn't have an immediate response to that. She found it quite satisfying that she had been able to shut him up. "Michael, I lost you once, twelve years ago. Granted it was to England, which makes it a much less bitter pill to swallow. But if I have learned anything over the past few days, it's that my feelings for you never died. They have only been dormant, waiting for you to awaken them again."

He reached up behind her neck and gently cradled the back of her head. "Then by all means, let me disturb their slumber." He brought her mouth to his and proceeded to give her a long, languorous kiss that warmed her all the way through.

When they parted, she found it difficult to catch her breath. "Oh, my."

He traced her lips with his thumb. "My sentiments exactly," he said in a raspy voice. "You have no idea how long I have wanted to kiss you, Emily."

She smiled slyly. "I hope it was worth the wait."

"Oh, it was. It definitely was." Then he pulled back again, his expression clouding.

"What is wrong now?" Emily said, his sudden reticence causing her concern.

"I want you to be absolutely sure about this, Emily. If we decide to pursue this further, I do not want to keep our relationship a secret. I am tired of deception."

"Does this mean you are giving up spying?"

"Eventually. I have to speak with my superiors about it. I want to leave the business as safely as possible. I have other people to think about. My mother for one. And now you. Until I can figure all that out, I will have to keep my disguise, at least for a little while." He gave her a mischievous smile. "Can you imagine yourself on the arm of Lord Hathery, dandy extraordinaire? One of the most—if not *the* most—irritating men in London?"

She laughed. "I cannot think of anywhere I would rather be," she said, brushing his hair back from his face and letting her fingers trail down the side of his cheek. "But what about you?"

"I do not understand what you mean."

A sudden bout of insecurity attacked her. "How would you feel having me on your arm? I am not exactly the society ideal, physically. You heard Charles. I am too plump. I am fairly short. I do not compare with the beauty of my sister and brother. It is something I have heard all my life." She waited for him to respond. When he didn't, anxiety threaded through her. But she wouldn't hold anything back from him anymore. From now on they had to be completely honest with each other. "I doubt I will ever be svelte like Diana or most of the other women, Michael, no matter how hard I try."

"Oh, Emily," he said, his expression turning soft. "Sweetheart, I do not want you to be. I am attracted to you—every beautiful, curvaceous inch of you. To me, you are not plump, you are perfect the way you are. You are the only woman I have ever wanted, Emily. So as far as I am concerned, this topic is closed forever. Have I made myself clear?"

"Quite," she squeaked out, so pleased she could barely speak. He wanted her as is, faults and all. Not only did she feel loved, she felt lucky as well.

"Good. I am glad we settled that." He leaned back against the settee. He looked exhausted, but happy. "We will be the subject of quite a bit of gossip, I imagine," he continued. "Especially the first time we are seen together in public. Everyone in London knows how much you hate me—"

"Hate is such a strong word," she interjected.

"Oh, but so very accurate in this case. That issue alone give the gossipmongers loads to prattle on about. Now that I think about it, Lord Hathery has never accompanied a woman to any social function, save his mother. Most certainly everyone will wonder why he has suddenly, ah, changed his proclivities."

"Then they will just have to wonder, for I am looking forward to attending as many parties as possible. Escorted, of course, by the dashing, if overdressed, Lord Hathery."

Her words made him smile. He had such a wonderful smile, which she had rarely seen until now. Actually, she thought everything about him was wonderful.

"I can only imagine the look on everyone's faces," he said.

"Especially the Hampton twins," she replied. "They will be positively beside themselves with shock. I believe they had a wager over who would marry first, you or Lady Caleigh."

"Isn't she close to eighty?"

"Yes. She was the odds on favorite, if I recall."

He chuckled, then clutched his chest, but kept smiling. "Do not make me laugh."

"Afraid of having a little fun, Lord Hathery?"

He lifted his eyebrows wickedly and moved to kiss her again. "Not at all, Miss Dymoke," he said, his lips hovering over hers. "As a matter of fact, I plan on having as much fun as I possibly can. Starting right now."

Chapter Twenty

Five months later . . .

"There, there, Clarissa. Now, there is no need to fuss." Emily held her tiny niece tightly in her arms and continued to soothe her cries. She reached over and smoothed the dark shock of black hair sprouting above her forehead, the color so much like Lily's. The baby had Colin's features as well, especially his piercing blue eyes and plump lips.

She was absolutely perfect.

"Here," Colin said, reaching for his daughter. "You are not holding her the right way. That is why she is crying."

"Colin," Lily said, rising from her chair in the corner of the sitting room. Since delivering Clarissa three weeks ago, they had left Leton House and returned to London. The doctor had a been slightly off in his prediction of her due date, but that didn't matter. Lily had regained most of her strength since the birth, and had been a doting, yet practical mother—a good compliment to Clarissa's highly overprotective father. "Emily was holding her just fine. She is hungry, that's all." She took her daughter from Colin's grasp.

"Are you sure?" Colin said, still staring at Clarissa. "Perhaps it is something else."

"I am positive. Please, Colin, you must relax. Everything is fine. Clarissa is healthy; I am healthy. But if you do not stop smothering, you may drive us both round the bend."

"All right," he replied, looking contrite and a bit hurt. "I will take my leave then. I am sure I have some pressing business to attend to . . . somewhere." He paused to kiss the top of Clarissa's head as he left the room.

Lily sighed. "I am already forgotten, I can see. I suppose that is what happens to mothers, they fade into the background."

"Oh, bother." Colin said good-naturedly. He backtracked and gave Lily a rather passionate kiss. "Satisfied?"

She grinned. "Very."

Emily watched her brother and sister-in-law with amusement. She understood Colin's fears. They had all been extraordinarily careful with Lily during the rest of her pregnancy and after the birth, which had also been difficult. But they all seemed to be getting into a routine, and Emily had no doubt her brother would settle down soon enough.

"I will be back shortly," Lily said, excusing herself after Colin left. "It won't take too long to feed her."

"That is quite all right." Emily stood. "I need to return home anyway."

"How are the wedding plans coming along?"

"Smashing. I think we will have everything in place for the ceremony next month."

"Wonderful." Lily kissed Emily's cheek. "Give your mother and Diana my best."

"I will."

Colin accompanied Emily to the front of the hall. "I still cannot believe that my baby sister is getting married. And to her greatest enemy, to boot."

Emily stuck her tongue out at him.

"Mature as always," Colin said. Then he did something unexpected. He kissed her on the cheek. "I am really happy for you, Emily. Michael is as fine a chap as they come. I know he will take good care of you."

Colin's butler, Bonham, handed Emily her wrap and gloves. "Thank you, Colin. That is very sweet of you. I am glad to know I won't be a burden to you anymore."

"For the love of—Emily, that is not what I meant . . ." His voice trailed off as he realized she was teasing. "God help Michael," he muttered, helping her into her coat.

"Lord Chesreton, your presence is required in the kitchen," Bonham said, looking a little frazzled. His spectacles perched low on his slender nose. "I believe the cook and maid are about to come to blows."

"Again?" Colin gave Emily a short wave. "I will see you soon."

After Colin left to referee his employees' latest spat, Emily wrapped her coat tightly around her body and put on her gloves. It was quite chilly out, and even though the distance from Colin's to her house was short, especially when traversed in a carriage, she still wanted to protect herself from the cold. She waited for Colin's vehicle to arrive and take her home.

There was a quick rap on the front door. Then it opened. Emily had just been thinking it was quite rude of someone to barge into her brother's home unannounced until she realized it was Michael.

He walked inside, held up his quizzing glass and peered down at her. "Miss Dymoke," he said, then took a deep bow. "I am most pleased to see you."

She felt a familiar tickling sensation in her belly, one she experienced every time she was around him. It always filled her with pleasure. "And I am pleased to see you. May I ask what has precipitated your unexpected arrival?"

Lowering his quizzing glass, he glanced around. "Are we alone?"

She nodded, then giggled as he grasped her by the waist and pulled her close, dropping his foppish façade. "Michael!" she said in weak protest. "Colin could walk in at any moment!

"A moment is all I need." He bent down and kissed her deeply, making her toes curl inside her shoes.

London society had been caught off guard when Lord Hathery and Emily Dymoke had announced their engagement a month ago. Nearly every single member of the peerage, save for their family, didn't understand how they could have changed from bitter enemies to a betrothed couple. At first they had suspected it was an arranged marriage, especially in light of Lord Hathery's fastidious demeanor and the fact that he was the last member of his family. But Emily soon put those rumors to rest by expressing complete devotion to her future husband. Before long the relationship that had caused so many whispers and raised eyebrows had eventually become accepted. Some even wondered if the mismatched couple knew something the rest of the *ton* didn't when it came to love.

Michael broke the kiss and set Emily back on her feet. "I couldn't wait to see you," he said huskily. "I stopped by your house, but Diana said you were here. I thought you might want an escort home."

"But I have Colin's carriage."

"He won't mind. It is a lovely evening for a walk."

Before long, Emily and Michael strolled along the sidewalk to her house, enjoying the crisp air and each other's company.

"I have news," he whispered, returning to his disguise despite them being alone on the street. He smoothed one eyebrow with the tip of his pinky finger. "I have heard from my superiors."

"You have? Do not keep me in suspense, Michael. What did they say?"

"I will be released from my duty shortly after the wedding."

"That is wonderful news!"

"Yes, it is. I will finally be free, Emily. However, I think it would be wise for us to leave London for a while."

"Why?"

"I cannot simply go back to my life before and change my entire persona in such a short time."

She understood what he meant. He wanted to start over, and he couldn't in London. He needed to be where no one knew him. He needed time to find himself again.

He halted his steps, causing her to stop. They were only a few feet away from her house. "I know I am asking a lot of you, Emily. I am asking you to leave your family. The only life you have ever known. There is still time to change your mind. I will take the blame if you want to break our engagement."

Emily sighed. She and Michael had come a long way in their relationship in the past few months. However, it was moments like these where he seemed to take six steps back from any forward progress he had made. "Michael, when will you ever learn?"

He raised a quizzical eyebrow. "What do you mean?"

"I love you. I love you with all my heart and soul. If you asked me to go to the wilds of India I would follow you there."

"I am unaware of any wilds of India." His lips twitched.

"You know what I mean. Wherever you are, that is where I will be."

He bent and kissed her again. "Have I mentioned how lucky I am to have you?"

"Not lately, no. I believe it is time for you to say so again."

Laughing, he kissed the tip of her nose. Then he

escorted her back to her house. Before she went inside, he said, "I was thinking about going to America. Are you up for a trip across the Atlantic?"

"Let me check my calendar, but I believe I do not have anything else planned. So yes, I would love to cross the Atlantic with you. Or the Pacific. Or any other ocean. As long as you promise me one thing."

"What is that?"

"We will always have fun. No matter where we are, we will have fun."

"It is a promise. I might even throw in a disguise or two, just to make it interesting." He pulled her into his arms as she laughed. "I love you, Emily. I love you so very, very much."

"I know." She kissed him with as much enthusiasm as she could muster. "I love you, too, Lord Hathery."

"Michael," he said, pulling her even closer.

"I love you both," she replied, kissing him again under the silvery light of the London moon.

Printed in Great Britain
by Amazon

58549328R00118